THE CHILDREN OF DUNSEVERICK

VIVIENNE DRAPER

BRANDON

First published in 1994 by
Brandon Book Publishers Ltd,
Dingle, Co. Kerry, Ireland

British Library Cataloguing in Publication Data is available
for this book.

ISBN 0 86322 195 5

Typeset by Brandon
Cover design by The Graphiconies
Cover painting: *Evening, Ballycastle, c. 1924* by Frank McKelvey
Drawings by Terry Myler
Printed by ColourBooks Ltd, Dublin

for my grandchildren

Contents

Children of Dunseverick   9

Journey to Dunseverick   15

Babies   25

A Little Matter of a Fence   31

The Scourge   37

Missionaries   43

Aunt Lily   47

Snobs and the Landed Gentry   57

Big Hugh   65

Father's Tales   71

Gypsies, a Christening and Rhymers   79

The King's Head   85

Red Herrings   93

Snowberries and Castor Oil   103

Story-telling, Ghosts and Ghouls   109

Aunty May and the Witch   123

The Threshing   137

The Boat to Rathlin   143

Bessie's Wedding   147

Epilogue   159

Children of Dunseverick

IN ADULT LIFE, while rearing a family of my own in Belfast, I returned to the scene of my childhood with my sister Philippa, who was visiting after twenty years in America. We took the coast road and had the sea on our right all the way up to Ballycastle. On we went through Ballintoy and Whitepark Bay, Portbraddon and then the little village of Lisnagunogue where Dunseverick Church stood, a plain grey stone building with a square tower.

'Nothing remarkable about it,' I said, perhaps a little deflated by its ordinariness.

'Except the sermons,' Philippa giggled, 'and the people. There were some great characters.'

'And Mother and Father,' I agreed. 'They were quite a couple when they were young.'

We drove through the village, remembering cottages, the shop that sold everything, the one pub. It still had only the one pub. Once outside the village we could see the house, and then when we arrived we just sat at the gate in the car, looking at it.

'Remind me,' Philippa said. 'I've been away so long. If it hadn't been for your letters I'd have forgotten altogether. Remind me.'

'I will,' I replied, 'but first let's go and look at the house.'

The grounds were neglected and there were gaps in the avenue where trees had been blown down by the frequent winter gales, but through one of the gaps I could see Rathlin Island, lying peaceful on this sunny October day. For some reason I found myself thinking of it in winter, veiled in fog, its horn moaning at regular intervals, the two red lighthouse eyes a warning to sailors and vessels abroad in that turbulent stretch of the Atlantic.

The house was no longer a rectory, for the economic necessity of amalgamating parishes had rendered it redundant. The church had now leased part of it to four young men who worked on a local newspaper. I knocked on the door to ask permission to look around, but there was no answer. I hoped they wouldn't mind our invasion of their privacy as we peeped through the windows of what had once been Mother's drawing-room. The young men obviously used it as a living-room, and it was comfortably furnished with lots of books. As yet there were no curtains on the windows; the house being so isolated they may have felt there was no need for them. I thought of Mother's tapestry curtains with the big brown curtain poles and the swish of the rings when they were drawn. The tall white marble fireplace was gone, in its place a modern heater.

We gazed in silence, overwhelmed by memories.

'Mother was so beautiful,' I said at last. I could see her, tall and dark in a green silk dress, twirling round that very room. Mother was very pretty and always kept the figure of a girl in spite of her pregnancies. She wore her gleaming dark hair in a bun at the back, or in two neat little cartwheels over her ears; it was luxuriant when long and loose after she had washed it.

'Poor darling pretty Mother,' I sighed, 'she hadn't much fun, and that terrible illness – rheumatoid arthritis. Nobody seemed to know anything about it in those days. Maybe that's why I've been thinking of her

so much lately – I've got arthritic aches all over me.
She'd be an angel of sympathy.'

We came to the back of the house and there was the
old coach house, just as it had always been. Gingerly
we approached the stairs that led from the coach
house to the loft above: they were surprisingly firm. It
was fifty years since Father had kept a pony trap here,
and eventually his first car. We climbed to the top of
the stairs and pushed the door open to loud creaks as
cobwebs tore and shrivelled. We stood in the doorway
looking down its long length to the window at the far
end that Father had put in to overlook Rathlin. He had
been a great man for a view. The room was full of
shadows. I remembered the lighthouse beam that used
to light up the loft wall on dark winter evenings while
Philippa and I pored over mathematics, algebra and
geometry at a deal table scored with our doodlings.

This dusty old room, with the bricks showing
through the plaster and a hole in the floor so that we
dared not enter, was where we had been taught our
earliest lessons. Our father, having been a teacher, had
decided that rather than send us to the National
School where head lice were prevalent, he'd teach us
himself. It had been generally accepted that as
Chairman of the School Board he knew what he was
doing. And he was the rector of the parish of
Dunseverick. A large, roundish man, he wore a gold
watch chain across his clerical grey waistcoat, and was
known for miles around as having 'the gift of the gab'.
He also did a bit of tutoring of the dissolute sons of the
landed gentry, spoiled brats with too much money and
no ambition, boys of whom their families despaired. He
was a strict disciplinarian though, and if they stuck it
some of them did well, got entrances to Trinity College,
Dublin, or to Oxford or Cambridge. Others went off as

far as they could go and joined the French Foreign Legion, or became mercenaries in anybody's war. In between teaching these adult pupils Father had endeavoured to come down to our level and teach seven and eight year olds. He hadn't succeeded, for he could neither coax nor cajole and he had no patience. He just roared at us and frightened us out of wits.

Philippa and I looked at each other. The years rolled between. 'D'you remember the scholarship he entered us for?' she whispered.

'Oh God!' I cried, 'I must have got those minimum marks for my nice writing. Remember he did teach us his beautiful copperplate handwriting.'

'We were constantly disappointing him ...' Philippa's voice trailed off.

'Yes. It's only with hindsight that we know it wasn't our fault. We'd have got the basics at the National School even if we'd got head lice as well. I have the most awful trouble with the multiplication tables even yet, and as for long division and fractions I haven't a clue!'

'You don't have to twist your brains into knots nowadays anyway,' Philippa said, 'what with computers and calculators.'

'However did we manage – you all those years in America? We were so unsophisticated and vulnerable, so country green.'

'I think I must have had a guardian angel,' Philippa smiled. 'Perhaps it was him, Father. Remember how frightened of the world he was for us? He wanted to protect us. But you survived too.' She looked through the dusty window to the sea and the island. 'There was so much beauty in those days.'

'I got through with a lot of bluff,' I replied, 'and the great love of literature he imparted to me. Remember those evenings in the study, sitting on his knee by the fire, him reading Dickens to us, and Shakespeare, Sean O'Casey and Synge. And the poets! Oh, remember Tennyson's "O sweet and far from cliff and scar The horns of Elfland faintly blowing!" And do you remember *The Pilgrim's Progress*? How I loved the description of "the delectable land". Look, there it is.'

I pointed to the fields, little green, yellow and brown squares and rectangles, and some with no shape at all. There were tall unkempt hedges as boundaries, here and there fences with homemade gates of old iron bedsteads. From clumps of trees obscuring gable-ends smoke rose from hidden chimneys. And away beyond, the purple shape of Knocklayde; the hill of the fairies we called it, though its name meant, prosaically, 'broad hill'.

'You always were a romantic. Look at all those TV

masts in the village; I'll bet nobody is as green as cabbage nowadays. Come on. I've had enough of old and fusty things.'

Philippa was half way down the stairs.

We descended to the yard, pulling the old doors shut behind us, closing out the view of Rathlin and the sea and the bitter-sweet memories.

On the way home Philippa said, 'Remind me. All those years – my memory isn't as good as yours. What made Father come so far from Dublin? Sure, he thought there was no place like it. Go on, tell me. Write it if you like.'

Like all Americans she was anxious to know her roots. And before she flew back I promised her I'd write it all down.

Journey to Dunseverick

BEFORE HER MARRIAGE Mother, then Constance Mary Garland, had lived with her parents, sister and three brothers in a cottage in the main street of Blessington, County Wicklow, where a huge chestnut tree stood in the middle of the square. A cottage garden ran down to a stream at the back of their house, and steep little stairs ran up to bedrooms from inside the living room.

Mother had lost one of her brothers in the Great War. He had been gassed and was brought back from the front to England where he died. It had broken his mother's heart, thinking of him lying in an English military hospital, not even able to write to her, and when the War Office had told her he was dead she had put on black mourning clothes and never again wore anything else. She only came once to visit us in Dunseverick; a timid creature, she didn't stay long, and the journey having proved too much for her she never came again.

Mother's father had been a cattle and horse auctioneer and could have made them all rich had it not been for the drink, of which he died an early death. One brother returning from the war went back to England, and one stayed to look after his mother. The two girls went to Dublin to train as nurses but were so homesick and frightened of the city they came home after a month. Aunty May met and married a tall, handsome man who played the cello and went to live in Kingstown (now Dun Laoghaire).

Mother had been glad to play the organ for a small salary in the church. And it was there that she met the new curate, Albert Oswald Draper. He was good looking and great fun, and all the girls around set their caps at him. Mother was too shy to do so; he noticed, and decided she was the one for him. He went up to Dublin and bought a ring, a pretty row of diamonds in a gypsy setting of little loops of gold, and it cost him £27. He asked her to marry him as they sat under the big tree after church on a Sunday evening. It was 1918. Mother wouldn't have dreamed of saying no, she told me later, and the whole village was delighted for her. So was her sad, dispirited mother.

Shortly before their wedding, Father received the news of a new appointment. He had a reputation for being good with young people, getting sports clubs and youth groups organised, and his gifts were wanted in a larger parish.

'They need you in Belfast,' the bishop insisted. 'Blessington is too small.'

Father was game for the challenge but he was worried what his fiancée would think. But she agreed to make the move as soon as they were married and even to spend their honeymoon in Belfast.

They were married in Dalkey in the spring of 1919.

'What did you wear, Mammy?' I asked her many years later, hoping for an account of flowers and frills.

'A navy blue suit,' she replied, 'and a white straw hat with a blue ribbon round it, and a new purse.'

When they arrived in Belfast in the parish of St Luke's in Townsend Street, off the Shankill Road, they moved into a great barrack of a house on the Ballysillan Road which later became the Victorian Homes for children.

'We only lived in half of it,' Mother said; 'we hadn't

16

enough furniture for the rest. It was a horrible place to spend our honeymoon.'

Father had been born in Harold's Cross, Dublin, and later his family had moved to Blackrock, to a house next to the railway line, beyond which lay Merrion Strand. His brother Vivian and sister Lily, his mother Isabella and Thomas his father, all lived happily there until one day the boys went gathering shellfish along the strand. Their father, who worked as a clerk in Guinness's, came home to a feast of boiled shellfish. He ate a plateful, became ill and soon afterwards died of typhoid. None of the rest of the family got it, though they had eaten the shellfish too, but the doctor said the shellfish had been the source of the disease. The boys, who blamed each other, felt an unbearable guilt for a long time. It affected my father the most – perhaps it was he who had instigated the gathering of the shellfish.

He always looked after the family after that. His mother was given a small pension by Guinness, but they had to sell the house in Blackrock and move to a rented one in Kent Terrace, Dalkey. Father urged his brother Vivian to do some training and paid for him to learn to become an electrician, after which he landed a job in Dublin Corporation. It was easier for Father after that.

At the time Father himself was a teacher; he taught Latin – which was his forte – mathematics and physical education in various Dublin schools. He lived in digs in the city and loved the theatre so much he often pawned his best suit or his books in order to go to the Abbey or the Gate.

'I always got them back again before the expiry date,' he told me. 'Teachers' salaries were not very good in those days. We used to lend each other things to pawn at the weekend, then get them back the following week. But I was very angry when a fellow took my Bible to pawn without permission. I expect he knew I wouldn't do such a thing with a Bible.'

It was then that he decided to go into the Church. He went back to Trinity to study for a degree in Theology and lived there in Botany Bay, teaching part-time and tutoring at night to keep himself in funds and continued to support his brother and sister. His mother had died by this time, in her nineties; his sister Lily looked after Vivian, and my father when he was at home. The two brothers refused to let Lily meet any eligible men, locking her in her bedroom when any of their friends came to the house, afraid of having to look for as good a housekeeper.

In later life I asked Father how they could have been so cruel.

'What'd she want to get married for!' he protested, 'with two of us to look after her.'

'But you got married!' I exclaimed.

'Ah well, that's different,' he replied lamely, 'she still had a brother. Vivian was a born bachelor. They were content together.'

When parish duties permitted it, Father always loved to take a trip down to Dalkey to make sure his brother and sister were all right. He'd take me with him. I loved the Dalkey house, which had a long passage from front to back with rooms on either side. There was a wild garden full of overgrown roses and cats, lots of cats. Aunt Lily adored them and encouraged all the strays in Dalkey to come and feast in her kitchen. There would often be two or three cats snoozing on the old Aga stove. Long years later when Aunt Lily was dead, Uncle Vivian kept a brown enamel jug on the Aga alongside the cats, or their descendants. The jug was full of strong, dark, sweet cocoa which he loved. I thought it revolting and oily, and slightly sour, but still I had a hard job getting him to accept my refusal.

More than once he would suddenly say, 'Excuse me a minute,' and slip out of the house, leaving me there with the cocoa and the cats. Then he'd come back with a huge box of chocolates and present it to me with gentlemanly grace. He was well known about Dalkey as something of an eccentric, especially after his sister had gone and he missed her care and attention. He became unkempt, shabby and unshaven. I asked him to come up to Belfast and live with me and my family, but he said he'd miss Dalkey too much, and with a twinkle added that he'd only get caught in a hail of bullets. No longer able to look after himself, he went to live in a home for old men run by the Protestant churches. It had 'Lunatic Asylum' engraved in the grey stone over its Victorian frontage and it gave me the creeps. He was warm and comfortable there but very lonely. He became more religious than of old, gave up smoking and looked askance at the bottle of brandy I brought him. I tried to coax him: 'A few little creature comforts at your age wouldn't do your soul a bit of harm'; but he just shook his head. When I visited him again I found that he had turned his face to the wall. He died soon after at the age of 94.

Mother survived the early years of her marriage in Belfast, but when riots broke out some years after their arrival in the parish she was truly frightened.

'Sure they're hurling the very paving stones at each other,' she wailed.

She'd had me and Philippa by that time and one day she took us and a case and went off back to Dublin on the train, and thence home to Blessington.

Father immediately requested a transfer to a country

parish and a sympathetic bishop obliged by appointing him to Seago parish, County Armagh, as curate, where his wife and children soon joined him. It was from Seago that he was transferred soon afterwards to Dunseverick.

Mother immediately loved the rectory of Dunseverick. It stood, solid and secure, at the top of an avenue lined by tall firs and laburnum trees, where clumps of daffodils and drifts of bluebells grew in spring.

The house was white with black wooden lace around the eaves; it had tall windows and six very tall chimneys which carried the smoke from the fires above the tree-tops. There was a big outer door, then an inner one with coloured glass; off the square hall were the drawing-room and dining-room on the right, on the left the study and the kitchen. Beyond the kitchen was a pantry and a wash-room where the Monday wash was done; the door to the wash-room was kept locked after

Philippa put her fingers in the mangle and turned the handle. At the back of the house in the big yard a lean-to outhouse literally leaned against the wall and housed 'clarendo' and other meal in sacks for the hens and goats. We often ate the clarendo, which was crunchy and flavoursome. Father said it would do us no harm but when a rat got in and ate holes in several bags Mother put her foot down.

Upstairs were four large bedrooms: Mother's and Father's, the spare room, and two which we children shared. A little one, which Mother said would eventually be Robert's, was a room in which Mother, who loved plants, grew Asparagus, maidenhair fern, and an Aspidistra. I envied the plants that little room and was jealous of Robert's inheriting it; I always wanted a room of my own, but Robert, being a boy, had to have it. 'He can't always sleep with girls,' was the only explanation I received.

On the lower landing there was another bedroom where Bessie slept and opposite was the flush lavatory, dependent on water being pumped up to the cistern from the pump in the yard. In the bathroom beside the lavatory was a big, deep, white bath that rested on four claw-like feet.

The rectory's long windows overlooked a variegated pattern of fields and hedges in the surrounding countryside, and there was a splendid view of the sea and Rathlin Island, which lay like a basking shark enjoying the even lap of the waves breaking against its chalk-white sides.

'We'll be happy here,' Mother said when we first arrived after our long journey from our home amongst the apples of County Armagh. And with our wonderful freedom to wander where we pleased, our childhoods were as happy as Mother had predicted.

There were five of us children, all born within ten years. Standing in a row for a photograph we looked like steps of stairs. I was the oldest and tallest; then came Philippa, one and a half years younger, who frequently worried me by stating that she was catching up with me both in height and age to claim first place as the eldest. She was almost my height but I didn't see how she could pass me in age. Nevertheless, it was often a bone of contention between us. Next came Helen and whereas Philippa and I had straight, dark hair Helen had golden curls and fair skin. She was the prettiest. Then came Robert, brown-eyed and dark-haired. When Mother was expecting her third child Father had wanted a boy and had the name Robert ready. 'Three times Robert the Bruce in his hide-away on Rathlin Island watched the spider climb its thread to reach its goal' was the way Father explained his choice of name. But his third try had been another girl. As Mother wanted a son too, they were both delighted when the fourth baby was Robert. And last came Jennie, fair like Helen, with grey-green eyes and a wide, smiling mouth.

We were usually dressed in tartan pleated skirts and hand-knitted woollen jumpers in winter, knee socks and laced up brogue shoes; fitted coats with velvet collars and berets completed our outfits. In summer the local dress maker, a Miss Campbell, made us dresses of bleached linen cut all in one like a doll's dress, the sleeves sticking out straight at right angles, and we hated them. When we bent our arms there was a great bunch of scratchy material under our arms. Mother dyed them pretty colours and embroidered them but they were still uncomfortable to wear. Miss Campbell was better at making Robert's trousers, neat little grey shorts with a pocket into which she always put a penny.

Mother loved perusing catalogues she got from
Manchester, and from these she close some of her own
clothes. One day she showed me a page of children's
clothes in it and I was thrilled to be allowed to choose
a pale green silk dress. When it arrived I put it on. It
clung to my thin body and when Father saw it he said
I looked like a caterpillar. Mother remonstrated with
him when she saw my crestfallen face.

'It's cheap-looking,' he said. 'After all, the children
have to sit at the top of the church in the rectory pew
for all to stare at. They should have good clothes. I'll
away to Coleraine. Tweedy Acheson's will have something suitable.'

He came back with twin sailor dresses for Philippa
and me, navy serge pleated skirts and blousons with
big white button-on collars. They had gold anchors
embroidered in the corners.

'Smart,' said Mother encouragingly, 'swanky'.

But when Father produced little round matching
sailor hats with 'HMS Ulysses' on them we rebelled.

'We're not sailors!' we cried.

Nevertheless we had to wear them to church next day
and several people admired us as we came out after
the service. We continued to hate these outfits: the
serge was heavy and as scratchy as the linen dresses,
and the hats were ridiculous.

Aunty May came to our rescue at Easter-time the following year by bringing us girls a present each of short
white organdy dresses with puff sleeves and satin
sashes. She brought Robert a real little shirt and tie.

'Expensive,' Mother exclaimed, 'all with labels from
Switzer's of Grafton Street, Dublin!' She held the beautiful garments up one by one. 'You are too generous,'
she told her sister.

'I heard about the caterpillar dress,' Aunty May whispered. 'An occasional little bit of femininity won't do any harm.'

Dunseverick was not a rich parish and so it was designated as a mere 'curacy-in-charge'. The parishioners regarded Father as if he were a full-fledged rector all the same. They were bewildered by him at first, but after a while they got to know him for a man with the gift of laughter and kindliness, and a fund of wonderful stories. They sized him up with a shake of the head: 'Ye're a terrible man, yer Reverence.'

For her part Mother was very active in the parish, riding her bicycle everywhere, playing the organ in church, organising the choir, and teaching the piano in the rectory. She took to Dunseverick immediately and the people of the parish welcomed her.

'With such a willing help and support as you, my dear,' Father said to her, 'we don't need a curate up here at all.'

Babies

THERE WAS AN air of great expectancy and excitement about the rectory when Mother was expecting her fourth child. After three girls, everyone wanted a boy. We were all up in our tree house when the midwife came. She was a grim-looking woman, big and strong, her navy serge cap hiding all her hair; we privately wondered if she had any hair at all. Spotting us on her way into the rectory with her bulging bag, she admonished us to keep quiet.

Father had built the tree house after spotting an abandoned cart in a farmyard with a broken shaft and no wheels. The farmer had transported the cart on a lorry and helped Father put it up in a chestnut tree with a wide bole, which stood at the top of the rectory lawn. The floor of the cart made a good strong floor for the tree house, and the sides, cut to fit, made walls. Father also made a sturdy little ladder and wedged it tight to where a red-painted door led into the house itself. The roof was the thick green leafy top of the tree.

When we had first seen our new domain we had been delirious with delight and had to have our tea up there immediately, bringing our treasures, dolls, books and a tea-set. Father, as enthusiastic as us, had made us a tiny table. Mother had donated a rug for the floor and let us have many a picnic there.

'Whatever you do don't fall down and break your necks!' admonished Bessie.

It was a magic place for us to play games, to keep house, or just to sit and read, the wind in the branches above us bringing the sounds of the sea.

We were still up in the tree house when, a lot later, the midwife emerged from the house. For hours now we had kept out of the way, whispering in our tree house about babies and where they came from and why Mother was in bed so often and always pale and tired.

'She's having the baby the same way the cows have calves,' Phil announced.

There was a sense of shock. I just didn't believe her. Hadn't Father told me to look under the bushes or ask the fairies when I'd asked him for a baby of my own? And, taking him at his word, I'd been gleaning the hedges for weeks, my eyes catching anything white nestling underneath.

'Who told you?' I demanded. She hung her head, reddening, then looked up defiantly.

'I read it in a little white book under Mammy's pillow,' she said; 'it was called *Before Baby Comes*.'

We sat in silence. It must be true, if it was in a book. Why did Father tell me that fairy story, I puzzled.

'Well, you know fairy stories are not really true,' Phil said pragmatically.

Suddenly a thought struck me. Sometimes a cow died, or her calf died. I began to cry, and Helen, only two years old, cuddled into me and cried too.

'There's a lot of blood,' I sobbed.

'She won't die, she won't,' Philippa was vociferous.

It was then that we spotted the nurse and scrambled down the wooden ladder. She paused on her way down the avenue when she saw us, all big eyes and tear-stained faces staring up at her.

'Has everyone forgotten you!' she exclaimed. Leaning towards us over the bicycle she said, 'You've got a baby brother! Go and see him.'

We began to run to the house, but I hung back.

'Mammy? Is Mammy all right, Nurse?'

'She's as right as rain,' the big woman smiled broadly.

'Was it like the cow? Does it hurt? Was there lots of blood?'

Her face darkened and she mounted her bicycle.

'Little girls shouldn't be asking such questions. It doesn't concern you till you're grown up. You'll learn soon enough then.'

In the rectory there was Father, all smiles, Bessie the maid carrying a tray up to Mother, and old Katie from the village, her arms full of linen for the wash, coming down the stairs full of pride after assisting at the birth of a fine son of the rectory.

Up in Mother's room there was the lovely smell of baby talcum powder and clean terry nappies airing on a towel rail by the bedroom fire. Beside the big double bed, in the cot we had all lain in when we were small enough, was a little pink baby with black hair.

'How do we know it's a boy?' I asked.

People smiled but didn't answer my question and Katie, back in the room importantly bustling about, said my tongue was too busy. I felt aggrieved; I didn't think my question unreasonable.

Later, when Mother was bathing the baby, she said that baby boys had different arrangements for going to the toilet and when the baby obliged with a demonstration all over the clean white bath towel I was quite satisfied.

'I only wanted to know,' I apologised.

'Of course,' agreed Mother, 'now come and hold him.'

Such happiness as I felt with that warm fragrant bundle in my arms is hard to describe. I sat in the bedroom window in a rocking chair that swung gently and looked over the fields to Rathlin Island, long and blue on a day of bright spring sunshine.

Mother moved about the room in her pretty flowered winceyette nightgown, singing to herself, preparing the baby's bottle from the tray of things Bessie brought up from the kitchen. Bessie leaned over me and the baby.

'He's gorgeous, just gorgeous,' she exclaimed, tears in her eyes.

'Don't you drop him now, child dear.'

I glared at her. Of course I wouldn't drop him. I even knew how to support his head in the crook of my arm. I'd watched Mother. And then there was Martha. She'd been working in the rectory when she'd had her baby on the kitchen floor, and everyone thinking she just had a sore stomach. Father had got her safely married to the father of the child. 'Far too young,' he'd said, 'but it'll work out all right.' And it had and she'd had twins the next time, and she always let me hold a baby. Our Bessie was just silly, I assured myself. I hugged my brother, pressing his soft cheek to mine, holding his tiny hand where the fingers were finding their way through the lace of his woolly shawl.

Father came into the room. He kissed Mother and whispered to her. They stood there, laughing and whispering while the fire crackled and I rocked the chair gently to and fro. The baby slept, and outside the first swallows swooped over the eaves of the house and the sea birds rode in from the sea to follow the plough turning a furrow in a brown field. Life stood still for one long second in the room. Then the clock in the hall chimed five strokes and Bessie called me to tea.

I'm not sure that I ever forgave Father for telling me such a story when I'd asked where I'd get a baby of my own. When Phil had told me the truth I'd felt silly. I asked Mother could I have one of my own and did it hurt a lot. She took my face in her hands.

'You can't have one till you are a big girl,' she said gently; 'your body is too small and it can't make a baby yet. When you are grown up and have a daddy for the baby you can have one. It hurts a bit but you don't mind when the baby comes.'

How I loved her.

A Little Matter of a Fence

O NE DAY MOTHER called me to go visiting with her, something I loved to do, my hand held in hers, chatting all the way.

We walked across fields of glebe land and along a little lane bordered by golden gorse, the colour and heady smell of which were rich and potent. Somewhere a lark was singing in the blue, cloudless sky above. Rabbits scuttled across our path. Soon I could hear the sea and I broke away from Mother and ran towards the cliff-top to catch sight of it.

'Come back, child, for God's sake!' my mother screamed. She stood stock still, her hands clasped, her eyes closed, frozen in her fright. I gazed from her to the sea which thundered on the rocks and over the spit of shingle far below, and suddenly I realised that one more step would send me tumbling over the edge. The whin bushes grew over the cliff-top, looking deceptively thick and solid, but the earth was crumbly beneath them and the roots bare. I carefully clambered back to my mother.

Grabbing my hand she hurried me to a farmhouse near by and banged on the door. A girl appeared drying her hands on her apron and opened the top half of the door.

'Missus dear, what's wrong?' she exclaimed, opening the bottom half of the door. 'Come on in.' Mother en-

31

tered purposefully, pushing me in front of her.

'Mary,' she announced, 'your uncle will just have to do something about putting a fence round that field.' She pointed dramatically at me: 'The child nearly went over!' And she swayed suddenly.

Mary rushed to her and helped her into a chair.

'Och sure, I'm never done naggin' at him, Missus dear,' Mary assured her. 'He's away to the harbour for fish, but he'll be back lookin' for his tea soon. I'll get at him. Now I'll make you a cup; you've had a bad fright I can see.' She pulled the black kettle over the hottest part of the peat fire. It swung gently on its chain and soon the lid was lifting as it boiled. She warmed and filled a brown teapot and set it to draw on the hob.

'When you think of how many lambs your uncle has lost over the years because of that dangerous place, it's hard to understand why it wouldn't be worth the expenditure to him.' My mother was recovering. 'What if a child goes over ...?' She shuddered again.

Mary put her hand on her shoulder comfortingly.

'I'll get at him again ... he'll have to do it ... I'll think of something, refuse to make him his food ...'

'I'll send my husband down if you think it'd help,' Mother sipped her tea.

'Aye, you do that, send his Reverence ... he'll have some ideas,' Mary sounded confident. 'It's not the money ... he has plenty, the ould skinflint ... says he's leaving it to me so long as I don't marry,' she laughed.

'And you such a lovely girl,' Mother scoffed, 'it's a wonder you haven't been snapped up already.'

Mary blushed, then laughed gaily again.

'Well, I'm very particular, taking my time.'

'Wise for your age, too,' Mother commented and handed her cup back. 'I feel much better. Now we must go. Come along, child.'

Mary pressed a paper bag into my hand. I knew it was more of the little cakes she had been plying me with.

'For the other weans,' she whispered, 'and come and see me soon again.'

'When the fence is up,' my mother said firmly. 'I wouldn't have a moment's peace otherwise.'

That evening in the study Mother told Father about the danger I had been in. The door was open and I crept in.

'I don't see what I can do,' my father said, 'that old reprobate McCann isn't impressed by anything, let alone a turned collar.'

'Can't you put the fear of God into him somehow?' Mother urged. 'The child was nearly over.'

They looked over at me where I had curled up in one of the big wing chairs by the fire. We were always referred to as 'the childer' or 'the weans' when there were more than one present, and 'the child' otherwise.

'I'll see what I can do; don't worry.' Father put his arm around Mother reassuringly. They looked nice, I thought, standing there close together in the firelight. I felt comforted and secure.

A week or so later I went with Father to a farm up the hill opposite the rectory where the sheep were being sheared. I felt sorry for the scaldy things that escaped the shearer's hold, so cold I thought they must be. In the big wool shed the wool was piled high, each coat sheared from its owner so skilfully it was almost intact. I saw Father looking at the piles of wool intently.

'Lend me that wool, will you, John?' he asked the farmer suddenly. The man was astonished.

'It has to go to the mill before it goes off,' he protested.

'Tonight'll do,' Father urged. 'Just for tonight.' He

lowered his voice as he explained what his intentions were for the wool.

'Right, ye're on, yer Reverence!' John slapped his knee as my father's plan emerged: 'I'll get the boys on the job right now while you go and get the fence man down. We'll need to be quick. I don't want me wool washed away be the tide.'

'We've all evening,' Father said. 'High tide's not till eleven tonight. I'm away for Dunlop and a contract for a fence. You make sure McCann's full now, won't you? Or as full as usual.'

'That'll not be hard,' John assured him. They both laughed heartily.

It was tea-time and we had to go home though my ears were all agog ... I knew something exciting was afoot.

It wasn't until the next day I heard Father telling Mother how Mary's uncle had been persuaded to put up a safe fence round the cliff-top at last.

Coming home from the pub in the village with the farmer John and Dunlop the contractor on either side of him to see he didn't lose his footing on the cliff path, McCann, well on in his cups, heard a sudden shout of alarm. The three halted as a man ran up from the shore towards them.

'Look at that there, McCann,' he shouted, 'yer sheep has all fell over.' And he pointed in the gathering dusk to the bundles of inert wool lying on the shingle below the cliff.

McCann peered drunkenly, then let out a bawl to awaken the dead, but not a sheep stirred.

'It's a fence you need,' Dunlop took his arm. 'Come on to the house till I get the details.' He patted his pocket where the contract he'd been told to bring was ready for signature.

That night in the study my mother sat on Father's knee and put her arms round his neck.

'It's a tarrible man y'are, yer Reverence!' she whispered in the vernacular of his parishioners, 'But I knew you'd think of something.'

The Scourge

SUNDAYS WERE DAYS of great importance in the countryside, not only for the rector and his family, but for all the parishioners; it was a day for meeting each other, a real social occasion as well as for its primary purpose. Father found he had a job on his hands to emphasise the fact that prayers and worship in a reverent manner took precedence over the news that Letitia Brown and Thomas Agnew had named the date for their marriage after walking out for eleven years. Letitia sang in the choir and Thomas sat where their eyes could meet, and they had ogled each other all that time without missing a single Sunday. One old man gloomily predicted that marriage would end all that excitement when they sat together as man and wife.

Mother played the organ for the choir and we all sat near her in the choir pews, the youngest beside her on the organ seat, so that she could keep an eye on us. Small fingers sometimes strayed, bringing forth a short impromptu descant on the organ. I loved sitting in the choir and watching the goings on of the choir members. One fellow made extraordinary faces – gurning I suppose it was. He'd do it unexpectedly at me and I'd be sick with suppressed laughter, nudged by Mother and glared at by Father. Fortunately the pews were high and I could disappear below and sit on a footstool clasping my stomach that was sore with giggling. Father lectured me about reverence in church regularly. Then a terrible thing happened.

A lively, spirited girl called Kitty, who sat directly behind my father, grew bored with the long service one Sunday, and she began during the prayers to pin the hem of my father's surplice sleeves to the back of the pew with thumb tacks from the choir notice-board beside her. I watched her, horrified and fascinated. She deftly reached for the wide sleeves which were draped across the top of the pew in front of her as he stood to pronounce the Absolution. When he went to move to the lectern to read the first lesson there was a tearing sound and he halted, turned slowly and saw the culprit. This was too much, I knew; it was the last straw. Making faces and giggling was bad enough but this was Irreverence with a capital I. Father's face went white, his eyes steel cold.

'Leave the church, Kitty,' he ordered quietly. She sat still, defiant. He repeated his order, louder this time.

Mother was shaking. She leant across to Kitty. 'Go, like a good girl,' she whispered.

I thought I was going to be sick, and Phil was quietly crying while the other girls in the choir began sniffing and looking for handkerchiefs, the men embarrassed. Kitty looked at Mother for a moment, then stood up and began the long walk down the aisle and out of the church. She held her head high and some said she walked like a queen. 'Queen of the tinkers, for that's where she comes from,' said others unkindly.

Father was very sad: he was fond of Kitty, who was the illegitimate child of a woman who worked a small farm far up the hillside. Later he went to see her, but her mother said Kitty was sick in bed. Father insisted that he see Kitty, and though she refused to speak to him, he was concerned when he saw her flushed cheeks and sweating forehead. 'I'll get the doctor,' he said.

It was tuberculosis. The doctor shook his head.

Kitty still refused to speak to Father though he visited her daily, bringing home-made dainties from Mother. We were not allowed to go with him, for TB was the scourge of the countryside and greatly feared. Then one night a messenger came for Father.

'She's worse, raving – come quick, yer Reverence, she's wanting ye.'

The man had a horse and trap and I watched as they galloped down the rectory avenue and away along the road until they were hidden between the high hedges of hawthorn and fuchsia.

'Poor Kitty,' I thought and vowed I'd never giggle in church again nor ever look at the fellow who made such awful, fascinating faces. Somehow I felt guilty – maybe I had encouraged Kitty, even though she was a big girl and I was only young, huddled on my footstool

beneath the pew, 'in convulsions' as my mother put it to Father. 'You are the rector's eldest daughter,' he'd said sadly to me.

Kitty died, aged seventeen. Father was sad for a long time and things were very quiet in church. Some people were angry that he had sent her out of the church that day. But one Sunday morning he told the congregation that when Kitty had sent for him that last winter night when I saw the man with the horse and trap come for Father she had wanted him to help her say the Confession, especially the lines 'We have offended against thy Holy laws,' and 'We have done those things which we ought not to have done,' and have him pronounce the Absolution – 'He pardoneth and absolveth ...'

'Now I will get well,' she had laughed gaily with something of her old spirit. But her eyes were too bright and her cheeks too unhealthily red. The scourge had got her.

Shortly after her death I developed a small swelling in my neck. Mother and Father hovered over me, their faces anxious. The swelling got bigger, but I didn't feel ill; in fact, I had never felt better, perhaps because I was now the centre of attention. Then one day Father took me on the bar of his bicycle to the doctor in Bushmills. It was a great treat to ride so with Father, safe between his arms. He was very fit and hardly ever had to dismount even going up a hill and he could pedal fast. After the initial climb from the rectory to the top of the hill we flew like the wind down the long slope to the Causeway crossroads, known locally as the Fingers, and arrived past Runkerry and the MacNaughton estate into Bushmills.

Dr Hughes took a look, prodded the swelling and an-

nounced cheerfully, 'We'll soon get rid of that.' He went and rummaged amongst what I thought sounded like cutlery in a drawer, and a young woman in a white coat boiled a kettle. I was laid on a trolley and Father held my head and said encouraging things. The girl in the white coat held my legs. I wasn't going to kick her, I said to myself. Dr Hughes came forward with a bright little knife and put some ice cold stuff on my neck. He made a quick little incision and I lay quiet while he squeezed and cleaned and made cheerful comments, put in a stitch and wound a long white bandage round my neck, Father holding my long hair up for him. I was lifted down from the trolley and we all went into the doctor's dining-room where he poured Father, who was as white as a sheet, a glass of brandy. He had one himself and joked with Father to help him recover. As if to remind everyone that it was I and not my father who had gone under the knife, I promptly fainted and fell out of the chair in which they had deposited me. The doctor waved his glass of brandy beneath my nose and had me sip it; I spluttered and coughed but I revived and soon felt better.

'Come on ... I'll buy you a slider,' Father comforted me when both of us had fully recovered. I enjoyed the wafer sandwich of cool ice-cream.

Nevertheless, the ride home on the bicycle was not as much fun as coming had been and I fell into the comfort of Mother's anxious waiting arms with tears of relief.

Phil developed a swelling too but her 'operation' was conducted in the Cottage Hospital in Coleraine, and bovine tuberculosis was diagnosed. It had come from cow's milk, which we drank unpasteurised, but we were healthy children and Phil soon shook it off. Father nevertheless worried about it and decided to buy a goat, and later bought several others. Goat's milk was reputed to be safe from the tubercular bacteria. Tethered on long ropes, they grazed in the big field beside the rectory where he milked them into a big blue striped jug and made us drink it there and then, warm with bubbles. The bitter taste of it is with me still.

Missionaries

A LADY MISSIONARY who had been to China brought Mother a gift of tiny Chinese ornaments – a pagoda, a little bridge, figures of pretty people wearing kimonos and big round hats, and a delightful china cherry tree. She wore a kimono herself, of turquoise satin heavily embroidered in gold thread and, although she had fudge teeth and glasses and thin, scraped-back hair, she looked very elegant. I heard Father remark to Mother after she had gone something about making the best of the dress and she said he was a naughty man. Father liked a good-looking woman: more effective, he said, even in the mission field.

'You're incorrigible,' Mother sighed, and smiled reluctantly as she took the ornaments and ranged them along our drawing-room mantelpiece, where ever after they reminded us of our visitor and added an element of oriental refinement.

Other returned missionaries – a whole family of them – who came to stay at the rectory caused great excitement because they brought a lantern and slides to show us pictures from their journeys in Africa. Father thought the parish should have the chance to see the pictures too and he invited as many as could come to an evening in the coach house. He dragooned the men to help him and they borrowed chairs from all around as well as using our dining and kitchen chairs; one farmer arrived with a cartful.

Everybody wanted to come. Most had never been to a cinema of any kind. Food was provided, everybody donating home-made scones and cakes, and there was lemonade and tea galore. There weren't enough cups so relays of them had to be hurriedly washed in the rectory kitchen. But this was after the 'magic lantern' show when all was stimulated chat about the wonder of the African scenery, the strange animals and the even stranger people. I was fascinated by their dancing and in particular their faces and bodies painted in bright patterns and colours. I heard people refer to them as 'poor pagans' but I thought they were wonderful, especially the children, dressed in strings of beads and very little else. I decided then and there that I would be a missionary when I grew up. The only bit of the film I was frightened of was when a group of heavily decorated and feathered men danced a war dance.

This was accompanied by the beating of small round drums made of skin and played rhythmically and expertly by the missionary's sixteen-year-old son.

'Tom-toms,' he explained; 'they perform this dance to warn of danger.' I found the drumming curiously hypnotic and a little scary and it went on and on in my head long after I went to bed late that night.

In the summer of that same year I was awakened early one morning by a strange distant sound. My window was open and I could hear it above the singing of the birds. I leaned out and listened. It came from beyond the village, a regular rhythmic beat, heavy and menacing. I raced into Mother and Father's room.

'Daddy, Daddy, the tom-toms! They're coming, the pagans are coming!' The drumming was louder now. Mother and Father exchanged amused glances.

'Out of the mouths of babes ...' said Father, and he burst into laughter.

'It's the Twelfth of July, child, a traditional march commemorating old battles of long ago. Hurry now, get dressed and I'll take you to see the procession passing.

'Great drummers, some of these men.' He was dressing as he spoke. 'They beat those big drums, Lambegs they are called, until their knuckles bleed. There's enthusiasm for you. Come on, get the others up. We'll watch from the gate. They'll be on the way to Bushmills and on to Portrush for the day.'

Mother protested: 'It's only half past six.' But we were all awake now and racing down the avenue where we hung, wide-eyed, over the gate just as the procession came in sight. I recognised local men who, seeing the rector, touched their hats – round, hard, black bowler hats, the same as they wore to funerals. Bright orange sashes edged with shiny fringes adorned them and war medals decorated their chests. There was a man with no legs whom I had been frightened of until Father had told me he was a hero of a battle called the Somme, and he now passed by our gate in the little cart somebody had made for him out of a box and pram wheels. Dressed in his Sunday best, sash and medals, he pushed himself along with gloved hands on the pram wheels of his cart, looking as proud as all the rest.

When they had all gone over the hill we went back to the house where Mother and Bessie were frying a lovely breakfast of soda bread, eggs and bacon.

Aunt Lily

'YOU MIGHT AS well live in Timbuktu, Albert,' his sister grumbled to Father after the long journey by train from Dublin to Belfast, then by bus to Bushmills, there to be met by Father, Phil and me in the donkey trap and be taken the last two miles to Dunseverick.

She was tall and imposing, and not used to children. She looked at us uncertainly. She wore a black serge suit with a long jacket, a white silk blouse, black stockings and flat shoes, but this sombre attire was topped with a bright pink hat.

'That hat is a shock,' I heard Bessie telling Katie in the kitchen.

Aunt Lily had brought us presents, she said, tapping one of her cases.

'Thank you, Aunt Lily,' we said in unison, and she nodded approvingly.

'They've got good manners anyway.'

We couldn't take our eyes off the cases. We had to wait a long time while Mother and Father welcomed her to the rectory and showed her to the Lantern Room, which was the guest-room. Its tall window looked down the avenue of trees and had a strange, dark wallpaper with large yellow shapes all over it which looked like lanterns. The big brass bed had been made up with white linen sheets and starched lace-edged bolster and pillow cases, several freshly washed and aired white wool blankets, and a gold-coloured satin quilt and eiderdown. The fire was lit in the grate and the flowered tiles in the surrounding mantelpiece gleamed brightly.

'Fit for a queen,' pronounced Aunt Lily who was very fond of Mother. 'You have done me proud, Connie.'

We all sat down to the evening meal together in the dining-room and Father said Grace as it was a special occasion and to impress his sister. He didn't always say Grace because meals were not necessarily formal and we loved to have ours in the kitchen. Father was often called out or delayed by parish demands. Once, when a visiting cleric was with us, Robert was experiencing his first formal meal in the dining-room and when he heard Father saying Grace he whispered audibly to Mother, 'What is Daddy saying?'

Aunt Lily was very forthright. She looked longingly at her soup.

'Keep it short, Albert,' she admonished, 'I'm hungry.'

Meals were wonderful at the rectory, everything fresh from the surrounding countryside and bread and cakes all made at home. The country people were generous to a fault and loved to spoil their rector and his family. He seldom came home from visiting without his bicycle bag, a large pouch of leather slung over his cross-bar, being full to bulging. Vegetables, fruit, eggs and fish all came to our door and Mother grew vegetables and flowers in the garden. We had apple trees and gooseberry bushes, blackcurrant bushes and our own potatoes. Father was both a fisherman and rifle shot and brought home rabbits for the table, once a hare. Jugged hare resulted but it was too rich for us. We refused to eat it, too, because we had been told that it was very unlucky to shoot a hare. But Mother cooked rabbit to perfection with young carrots and parsley, chives and new potatoes and we never refused that. Harvest Festival dinners were a speciality, for then often a bishop visited and was put up in the Lantern Room. A great roast of beef was ordered from Bushmills and a special bottle of what Father called mountain dew was put away in the sideboard with the wine for Communion, and was to be used for 'medicinal purposes', mainly for keeping out the cold. It was often very cold indeed on that northern coast.

Mother cooked the roast in the big black range in the kitchen along with the potatoes, turned golden in the roasting dish, bright green Brussels sprouts from her own garden and cauliflowers smothered in creamy white sauce; all followed by apples bursting with sultanas and golden syrup. The grown-ups then had coffee with just a drop of that stuff out of the sideboard in it, 'to keep the cold out'.

Such was the meal Aunt Lily enjoyed, too, that night she arrived, and after eating she declared herself so full and satisfied that she'd have to go to bed early to sleep it off. We were afraid she would do just that there and then and forget to give up the presents she'd brought us. But she saw us waiting around the dining-room door in the hall and suddenly remembered the parcels on the hall table.

'There you are, children,' she handed out the parcels. I got a heavy square box. 'And here's one for Philippa ... where did you get such an outlandish name, Albert? And where's little Helen?'

Helen always got instant smiles and her present was something large and soft.

'And now the man of the house,' and Robert was handed a long box.

We rushed off to the kitchen while the grown-ups went into the drawing-room and Mother played the piano. Aunt Lily had a good singing voice and Father a wonderful baritone and soon the house was full of music.

In the kitchen with Bessie we opened our parcels. Mine was heavy, a large box of coloured wooden bricks of differing shapes, including bridges, turrets and triangles, squares and rectangles. I looked at it doubtfully. Phil uncovered a beautiful china-faced doll, its velvet dress edged with swan's down. I felt a pricking begin in my eyes. Helen unwrapped a soft, furry white cat with blue eyes and huge blue bow to match. She instantly loved it. Then Robert tore the paper off his box and opened it. Inside was a doll, a black doll with curly hair, earrings and a necklace, shining brightly coloured clothes and a smiling red-mouthed china face. 'Topsy', it said on the box.

We all stared in silence, the pricking getting worse in my eyes. Then Bessie said, 'She's made a mistake – that's it. The doll is for you, Vivien, and the bricks are for you, Robert – of course.'

She went to effect the exchange, but reckoned without Robert.

'No! No!' he shouted, 'I want the dolly ... She's mine ... she's mine ...'

'But Rob – the bricks will go with your train set, and you can make stations, sidings ...' Bessie reasoned.

It was no good. He held on to the doll, gazing at her, fascinated, gently inspecting her bright jewellery and exotic clothes.

I sulked and pushed the bricks away.

'Be patient,' Bessie whispered. 'He'll get tired of her.'

Mother was told of the predicament and, like Bessie, urged patience. 'Mustn't offend Aunt Lily now – be a good girl,' she said and went back to the drawing-room with a tray of glasses and fruit cake.

On the way to bed I lost the patience I'd been urged to have.

'Give me that doll, you little sissy,' I hissed, grabbing

the doll by her coloured skirts; 'boys don't play with dolls.'

But Robert clutched the doll by her curly hair. 'No! No! No!' he screamed, 'she's mine, my dolly.'

We heaved to and fro on the landing. Suddenly something gave and like a Christmas cracker the doll exploded in two. Robert was left standing with the curly hair in both his clutching hands and I had the scalped doll in mine. I looked into the china head and saw the mechanism that allowed her eyes to open and shut and the little china teeth stuck on to the smile, and suddenly it was ugly, obscene. With a scream I threw it over the bannisters, where it landed at the feet of Aunt Lily who was just then coming to say goodnight to us.

The other disaster of Aunt Lily's visit was the day she tried to cross the rope bridge. Carric-a-rede is a rock, a bird sanctuary joined to the mainland by a swaying rope bridge, and used by salmon fishermen. Father went across first, the bridge swaying alarmingly under his weight. We stayed with Mother on the land side, the whole day out spoiled for me by this episode. I hated any of my loved ones to be in any danger. We all shivered and clung to Mother. She refused to cross but Aunt Lily wouldn't allow her brother to outdo her. While he stood on the rock surrounded by indignant screaming sea birds on the far side and shouted encouragement, she started to cross.

'Hold your head up: look at me – don't look down!'

I hid my eyes in my mother's skirt but I knew that far below that fragile bridge the sea thundered on rocks that were like giant teeth waiting to gnash to smithereens the unwary and foolhardy.

'It's all right: there's only a little wind – come on,' Father called.

Aunt Lily got to the middle of the bridge, then froze. Like a tall statue she stood, her hands gripping the rails, knuckles showing white beneath the skin. Father encouraged her until he realised that she wasn't hearing him. He crossed to her and there the two figures stood facing each other on the bridge while the wind freshened and the waves thrashed the rocks, sending spray high enough to soak the two of them. We watched fearfully and saw Father prising Aunt Lily's fingers off the ropes, talking to her all the time. Then, holding her round the waist he made her turn slowly until she was facing us. Then he put his toes against the back of her heels and pushed each foot alternately so that she had to move forward. It seemed such a long time until they were safely on our side. Aunt Lily sat down promptly, white-faced and shaking, on the grass and Mother went to her while we hugged Father and tried to make him promise never to go on that bridge again. He wouldn't promise.

'It's a great place to fish from, but I'll promise you one thing. I'll never take your Aunt Lily on the bridge again.'

They didn't really get on, he and his sister. She didn't agree with his theology.

'The Church of Ireland's going all to pot,' she'd announce in her beautiful Dublin brogue. 'I think I'll join the Methodists.'

On the Sunday before she was due to return to Dublin she put on the shocking pink hat she'd worn on her arrival and went to church. Mother, being pregnant, wasn't feeling too well so she stayed at home to oversee the dinner, another grand one for the end of Aunt Lily's visit. Bessie did the cooking and we, who wouldn't go to church without Mother, set the dinner table. The windows of the dining-room overlooked the road to the church in the village. Suddenly we saw the shocking pink hat returning as Aunt Lily retraced her steps to the rectory, though it was only half way through the service. It transpired that she had disagreed with Father's sermon, had got up from the rectory pew and left the church.

'In front of all my parishioners!' Father fumed, and they argued all through the meal, hardly tasting it in their anger with each other.

Next day Father drove Aunt Lily with Phil and me in the trap to Bushmills. There was complete silence until the donkey stopped dead and refused to budge. Father stood up and whacked it with the reins, shouted at it, got long thorny branches out of the hedge and whacked it with them, but its hide was as thick as old leather and it hardly blinked an eyelid. Aunt Lily was beside herself, grim-faced with anger and frustration.

Then a car, one of very few in the district, drove up behind us. It was Dr Hughes from Bushmills. He stopped, took in our plight and laughed loudly.

'I told you that animal would let you down sooner than later,' he roared, 'as well as being an undignified mode of travel for the rector of the parish.'

'We don't all bleed the people white by overcharging for lancing boils and sewing up cuts with cat gut,' my father bawled back. 'Not to mention the cost of taking out appendix and tonsils, and a few teeth when the dentist's back is turned! No wonder you can afford a car!'

The doctor continued to laugh and I got the feeling that he and Father were good friends and were enjoying sparring with each other. After a few more exchanges Father explained the situation and we were thrilled to find ourselves and Aunt Lily transferred to the doctor's car. Father had to stay with the donkey and trap and try to get it going.

'I'll be back this way to rescue you,' the doctor called, and his laughter echoed in Father's ears as I watched out of the rear window of the car while he wrestled with the obstinate donkey. His lonely plight quite spoiled my pleasure in the car ride for a few minutes, but soon we were over the hill and could see in the summer sunshine the gleam of the sea all along the coast from the Giant's Causeway, past Dunluce Castle and the White Rocks at Portrush, the long strand at Portstewart and the misty blue shape of Donegal in the distance. I felt like a queen. Aunt Lily was quite mollified by the doctor's affable company and as we helped her into the bus for Belfast and saw her luggage stowed away safely she gave us each a shiny new half-crown.

'Be good to your mother, children – she has a lot to

put up with,' and she bent to whisper to me: 'I'll bring you a doll next time, dear.' I hugged her suddenly and she drew back, abashed. But she waved and smiled at us from the bus.

Dr Hughes shook his head. 'There goes a terrible waste of a grand woman.' I wasn't sure what he meant. He said he had a couple of short calls to make and bought us 'sliders' to enjoy while waiting in the car. We were so overwhelmed with the luxury of it all that we had no words, just grinned at each other and licked steadily, content as two cats who have stolen the cream.

Finally the doctor reappeared with a huge bunch of fresh carrots and we set off again. Over the hill once more we saw Father sitting exhausted and helpless in the trap while the donkey stood four-square and stationary, its ears flat down in obstinate anger. Laughing till he was bent double the doctor lifted the bunch of carrots and extracted one. He went to the donkey and proffered the bright orange bait. Instantly its ears lifted and the carrot disappeared into the capacious mouth and was crunched with evident enjoyment.

The doctor hooked the rest of the bunch of carrots by the string that held them to the back of his car.

'Watch this and hang on,' he admonished Father, and drove round to the front where the donkey was already looking for another luscious carrot. Then he drove off at a gradual speed, the donkey following. As the doctor increased speed, so did the donkey. We arrived at the rectory gate with the donkey at a gallop, Father bouncing up and down in the trap and holding on with difficulty to the reins. Convulsed with laughter, the doctor drove through the rectory gates and up the avenue, arriving with a flourish on the white gravel sweep before the front door. Father climbed down stiffly from the trap while we were handed from the car like ladies of importance by the doctor, and the donkey was taken off to his field to enjoy the rest of his carrots.

Snobs and the Landed Gentry

'**W**HY IS MAMMY crying?' I demanded, near to tears myself.

Philly didn't know and Helen stuck her thumb into her mouth and began to cry herself. Robert was in the kitchen with Bessie and Katie. The three of us burst in and I demanded again, 'Why is Mammy crying?' The two women looked, alarmed, at each other. Then Bessie came forward to me.

'Now listen, lamb,' she took my hand, 'you're a big girl. Ladies, Mammies, often have to have a little cry. Your Mammy wouldn't want to make a fuss ...'

'But why?' I insisted, my own tears pouring down.

'There doesn't have to be a reason, pet. You know your Mammy is going to have another baby – she's tired maybe. Tell you what, I'm making tea – you bring her up a cup on this nice tray, and Phil, you bring her some of Katie's hot scones. It's time for afternoon tea anyway, even if there aren't any visitors.'

I was very careful with the tray, glad that the two little ones had decided to play pirates-at-sea, a game that necessitated turning the deal kitchen table upside down. It made a great ship with its wooden sides and legs for masts and flags. Katie and Bessie supplied checked tea-cloths and yellow dusters for the pirates' headgear. Any other time Philly and I would have been wrangling over the captaincy, but today we were too engrossed in getting the tray ready for Mother.

'Here, just a minute,' Bessie opened the kitchen window and reached for a cabbage rose growing over it. 'There's a beauty for you,' and she put the full-blown rose in a small jug and set it on the tray. 'That'll cheer the missus up, poor dear sweet thing that she is.'

We listened outside Mother's door. The crying I had heard earlier had ceased. We opened the door slowly, still careful with the tea things. Mother was lying on the bed. She was pale and clutched her white handkerchief in her hand, but she turned to us and smiled, exclaiming, 'Oh isn't that nice? And just look at that rose! Did you two pick it for me?'

We'd have loved to say yes, but owned up grudgingly.

'Dear Bessie, she's so thoughtful.' And Mother buried her nose in the perfumed petals. 'Nothing like a cabbage rose for perfume. Thank you too for bringing up this lovely tray so carefully.' She patted the bed, 'Come here and have a scone. There are too many for me.'

Nothing loath, we had one each and sat on the end of the bed, munching and smiling contentedly at Mother, who wasn't crying now and had pushed her wet hanky beneath her pillow. After our tea Mother let us dress up in some of her pretty hats, gloves and necklaces.

'My, what swanks you are!' she laughed as I draped a chiffon scarf over my cotton dress and donned a cloche hat that came down to my ears and over my eyes. Philly, resplendent in a big wide-brimmed white panama hat, burst into laughter.

Such afternoons were as content as the promise of a summer day, and summers on that northern coast were as calm and balmy as the winters were stormy and cold.

Later that evening, still haunted by the sound of Mother's crying, I asked her why. She looked at me.

She had been talking to Father and now her eyes were brighter.

'I was being very silly. It was those visitors who came on Sunday ...'

'You mean, the new clergyman and his horrid wife and son?'

'Well, she's a formidable woman, haughty – he's not so bad really ...'

'He's not as good a preacher as Daddy.'

'Oh well,' Mother smiled, 'that'd be hard to be now. You daddy's a real orator.'

'And their son is ... ugh ... he's a real ... gooby,' I declared.

'What on earth is a gooby?' Mother inquired, laughing at my scowling face.

'It's soppy, and ... ugh, and ... just plain gooby!'

'Why is he that then?' Mother was curious.

'He's fat and he can't run, couldn't play a single game without a big fuss, and he cheated as much as he could. And then,' I lowered my voice, 'he pulled up my skirt!'

'Oh dear – he's a gooby all right!' Mother agreed.

'But,' I came back to the thought still in my mind, 'why did they make you cry?'

'They – well, it was Mrs Morrow-Smith – she made nasty remarks about people having too many children, like the Catholics, she said.' Mother bit her lip and continued almost to herself: 'Made me feel like a rabbit.'

'What's a Catholic?' I asked.

'Oh dear ...' Mother sighed; 'they're just another sort of Christian – like us but different,' she continued lamely. 'There are a lot of them down south where Daddy and I come from and up in Belfast, maybe in Portrush and yes, in Ballycastle. There aren't any living here, in Dunseverick. They believe in having children, their churches are called chapels, and they ...' she smiled, 'they're good fun.'

'Well,' I said, after a long pause in which I rested my eyes on her swollen tummy under the pretty, loose brown dress she wore, 'God only sent Mrs Morrow-Smith one baby, and it's a horrid rude boy, and he sent you all of us. I expect He thinks you're a really good Mammy.'

'Oh darling,' I was alarmed when she reached for her handkerchief again and dabbed her eyes, 'what a lovely thing to say.'

I glowed, warm and proud, in her embrace.

The Morrow-Smiths were in charge of a neighbouring parish, and Father perforce had dealings with them, as infrequently as he possibly could.

'Snobs, they are,' he pronounced loudly every time they visited.

So it was a very special day for him, and for Mother, though for him one to relish, for her it was tempered with chagrin, when my brother, then five years old, answered the door to the Morrow-Smiths' imperious knock and announced them in fine style as he had observed Bessie to do, as 'Mr and Mrs Snob'!

The landed gentry were a thorn in Father's side, and they frightened the wits out of Mother. She loved the fisherfolk and the villagers best, their kindly ways and honest eyes, their love of her and their way of life, simple and good, full of happy events and sad events, uncomplicated by any sophistication. The landed gentry were another kettle of fish. Father knew how to handle them.

'They're useful,' he said to Mother; 'we need electric light in the church, and old Lord Massingham'll maybe come across. He's going downhill with all the alcohol he consumes and is beginning to worry about his soul.'

Mother was shocked.

'You wouldn't let him think ...' she protested.

'If I can persuade him that putting electric light in God's house would be a better memorial to his life than the upkeep of the Bushmills Distillery, it'd go a long way to saving his soul,' said Father airily.

'I wish I could have electric light too,' said Mother wistfully as she crushed up newspaper and inserted a ball of it into a glass lampshade, twisting and rubbing, polishing carefully; 'this is a never-ending job.'

'That too,' Father said. 'Lord and Lady Hamilton were asking about that very thing. They're a nice couple, down to earth, gentleman farmers; work hard on their land, good to their labourers. He's on the vestry and was shocked that the rectory hadn't got electric light yet. Don't worry, the vestry are all for it.'

Before long Mother did indeed get her electric light, but she kept one little oil lamp just in case the wonderful new lighting ever failed.

Father had a clash with another titled lady. One day he was riding his bicycle past her gates on the way to Bushmills when her small white terrier dog shot out like a rocket and sank its teeth in his trouser leg. Fortunately it didn't draw blood and Father managed to shake it free and gave it a good kick just as its owner dashed out after it. She gathered the yapping terrier up in her arms, murmuring soothingly; 'talked bosh' to it Father reported afterwards; and she berated him soundly for his cruelty. Father told her she was lucky he hadn't been more injured because she would have had to pay enormous compensation; as it was his trousers were torn. He knew the Templetons were on their uppers, and his words struck home. Her face blanched and she retreated through the estate gates hugging her howling dog.

Later, however, she fashioned her own response in the form of an invitation to speak at the Annual General Meeting of the local branch of the Ulster Society for the Prevention of Cruelty to Animals. He laughed heartily on receiving this, and when the meeting arrived he had his speech ready. As an animal lover, he said, he was enthusiastic and as an authoritarian he advised all dog owners to keep their pets under control: 'Discipline is to an animal, as to a child, a safe and secure haven.'

Applause greeted his speech, and looking across the table to where Lady Templeton was sitting he saw her smile slowly and her lips move gently to form the word 'Touché'.

Father had a penchant for collecting old furniture and haunting auction rooms. He loved a bargain, and Mother often waited in dread of what would arrive after his visits to an auction. Sometimes he bought beautiful things, as were two pairs of heavy brocade curtains with poles and rings that clattered in the pulling to and fro, which hung in the drawing-room, and a mahogany tallboy that was as tall as the picture rail and had a green baize writing desk in the middle of it disguised as a drawer. But one day he bought and had delivered a set of six dining chairs with horsehair seats and a huge armchair in a blackish brown leather.

'I don't like them, really,' Mother commented, 'they're already shabby.' But they went into the dining-room where there was already a beautiful mahogany table he had bought at a private auction. The armchair he put in his study where it belonged immediately and could hold him and two of us easily at story time by the big fire.

Then one day the Morrow-Smiths – 'the Snobs', as we now knew them – came again for the day. It was an Advent Sunday and Father and the Reverend Morrow-Smith were exchanging pulpits. It was the custom to give the congregation a change of preacher two or three times a year, lest they grow stale on too familiar a diet of sermons.

Mother had a wonderful dinner for them, with a pre-Christmas home-made plum pudding, and we had laughed so much over Robert's mistake that she was quite relaxed. Then, as we took our places at the table, their son, Denis the Gooby as we called him, ex-claimed: 'Look, our chairs!' His father had the grace to admonish him, but he insisted, 'They are ... they are ... look, this is the one I didn't like, with the stuffing coming out ... it scratches my legs.'

There was an embarrassed silence, then Mrs Morrow-Smith tittered insincerely. Her husband or-dered his son to be quiet, at which Mrs Morrow-Smith rushed to the boy's defence.

'That's all right, pet,' she gushed, 'I'm sure a nice girl will get you a cushion.'

I will not, I whispered to myself, anxiously looking at Mother. To my relief she was laughing. 'Yes do, alana, please,' and she went on to explain Father's predilec-tion for auctions and how she never knew what he would bring home next. 'He loves a bargain,' she told them, quite at ease, and I noticed that Mrs Morrow-Smith wasn't quite at hers.

When Father returned and heard the story he was thoughtful.

'I made a mistake,' he admitted.

He took the dining chairs out to the top of the big

field beside the rectory and piled them up. Then he set alight to them. As the rectory was on a rise the smoke could be seen for miles around.

'Smoke signals? What message are you signalling?' asked the doctor coming on a routine visit to see Mother. 'And what are you burning those grand chairs for?'

'A bad buy I made, a bad buy,' my father shook his head sadly. 'They were full of fleas.'

Big Hugh

I WAS WAKENED one winter night by voices outside the rectory and I heard a window being opened in Mother and Father's room. I peeped out through my curtains and saw down below a huddle of village women with shawls over their heads against the cold. There was a big round moon shining above the tree-tops and though it was dark there was light all around. Father leaned out of the open window in his night-shirt.

'What ails ye, at this God-forsaken hour out of your beds?' he roared.

'Och yer Reverence, it's Big Hugh! He's drunk again and he's driven his wife and weans out of the house and they're hidin' in the graveyard. Och yer Reverence, it's a terrible thing ...'

'Indeed it is,' I heard Father shout down to them; 'have ye no wit at all! Why don't ye go and get the woman and her children and take them into your homes in all Christian charity instead of gibbering there at this time of night ...'

I heard Mother protest.

Then the women called again: 'Will ye not come yer Reverence, and see to Big Hugh?'

'Indeed I will not! A man in his cups is not a reason-able being. In the morning I'll be down, when he's sober, and I'll put the fear of God into him. I promise you,' his voice softened; 'go on home now and see to your unfortunate neighbours like good women. It's a blithering cold night.' The women began to move off down the moonlit avenue. 'That's it, there's good women. Good night now. I'll be down in the morning,' and he closed the window and went back to bed.

I heard Mother and him arguing. 'You should go, dear,' she urged.

'No, he's a bigger man than I am, a giant of a man he is,' Father was adamant.

'I'm not asking you to fight him ...' pleaded Mother.

'No, but he might want to fight me,' Father protested. 'I'll see to him in the morning. It's a waste of time when the drink's in him.'

Soon I heard him snoring.

But he did get up very early next morning and I saw him riding down the road to the village on his bicycle.

Big Hugh was a fisherman and he only drank heavily in bouts. Mostly he was out at sea making a living and his wife and family thrived well enough on his earnings.

After this particular bout when Father went to see him early in the morning, he was lying on the floor of his cottage. The peat fire was still smouldering, and so was Big Hugh. Father smelt the burning as he propped his bicycle against the cottage wall and pushed open the door. Immediately grasping the situation he rushed to the tap in the scullery and filled a bucket. Steam rose as he threw the water over Big Hugh, who groaned and thrashed about wildly. Father helped him up, his rough fisherman's jersey singed and smoking.

'Bedad, man,' exclaimed Father, 'you were nearly in kingdom come that time. Here, sit down ...'

Big Hugh began to come to a slow realisation of the situation as he smelt and felt the ruination of his jersey. His bleary eyes held something of awe as they squinted at my Father.

'Tell you what,' said Father jovially, 'I'll make a cup of tea ...'

'Where's Mary?' Big Hugh suddenly roared.

'Sure, didn't you chase the poor woman out into the cold night, and she in her night clothes ...' Father called as he filled the heavy black kettle in the scullery: 'Not to speak of the poor wee weans ...'

Big Hugh put his head in his hands.

'God save us, did I do that, yer Reverence?'

'Indeed ye did,' Father scraped the embers on the open hearth together and hung the kettle on its hook over them, 'but they're all right. Your good Christian neighbours have them safe and sound.'

Father lifted the bellows beside the hearth and blew the fire till it glowed and the kettle boiled. Then he took the brown teapot from a little corner shelf beside the chimney breast and filled it liberally from the tea caddy on the shelf and set it in the embers to draw.

'I know where Mary keeps the sugar and milk,' Father went into the scullery again; 'many's a fine cup the good woman has made for me.'

Big Hugh's hands were shaking as he took the enamel mug of strong hot tea from Father.

'The drink's a terrible thing, yer Reverence.'

''Tis so,' Father agreed, sipping his mug of tea.

'Aren't you goin' to say somethin' ... somethin' out of the Bible maybe ...' Big Hugh's voice was urgent.

'No,' said Father.

'And me near death's door ...' Big Hugh raised his voice then trailed off as more realisation dawned, 'and you saved me.'

'Aye, another minute and you and the whole shootin' match would have been up in flames.'

'How'm I goin' to thank you?' Big Hugh was in earnest.

'Depends ...' Father said thoughtfully.

'On what?' Big Hugh asked eagerly.

'On whether your life was worth saving,' Father paused. 'Think on it.' He picked up his hat, 'I'll leave you now and I'll send Mary and the childer over. Be kind to them.'

He turned as he stooped in the low doorway: 'Remember now, and think on it. I'll be back.'

One surprising outcome of this meeting of Father and Big Hugh was that they became great friends. Father often went out with Big Hugh and his crew to fish, and he'd come home loaded with fish, several times clutching a lobster.

We thought it was so cruel to see him put the lobster in a big black pot of boiling water alive and frantically waving its legs.

'Kill it first, Daddy,' we pleaded.

'How?' he exclaimed; 'pull off its legs one by one? One way is as bad as the other. Wait till you taste it, though: lobster is succulent, delicious.'

We were not impressed, finding it impossible to reconcile ourselves to the sight and sound of the unfortunate shellfish, and he took to going home with Big Hugh when they caught a lobster and cooking it there.

Big Hugh gave up the drink, and came to church – even enjoyed it, he said, especially when Father preached his 'evils of strong drink' sermon. He sat at the end of one of the pews and chewed tobacco, spitting the black juice through the filigree ironwork that ran each side of the aisle over the heating pipes. Mother said his new habit was nearly as reprehensible as the old one.

Some years later there was a terrible storm one night and the banshee was heard in the village, her plaintive wailing cry heralding a death. Everybody cowered in their homes. The storm did damage everywhere, blew down trees, lifted corrugated iron roofs off sheds, and uprooted fences; the rain that fell like batons filled the dikes and shoughs to overflowing. Like a wild witch the storm raged over the countryside and then there was a lull. But it was only a lull. Suddenly it blew up at sea, hurling grey walls of thunderous water at the fishing boats that had ventured out to earn their living.

Big Hugh and his crew were drowned that night and my father's voice was full of tears for his parishioner and friend as he sadly conducted the burial service in the old graveyard by the sea.

Father's Tales

MOTHER AND FATHER had been invited to a special occasion and we were to have our dear friend Jane from the village to sit with us for the evening. Our excitement matched Mother's. She had a new dark green silk dress she had sent for from Manchester out of a Ponting's catalogue. It had a flare at the back and we made her twirl so that we could admire it. She had added a Carrickmacross lace collar and cuffs and she wore dark silk stockings and patent leather shoes with silver buckles on them. Her dark hair was knotted in a soft bun at her neck.

'Oh Mammy, you look beautiful!'

Father was all dressed up too, in a frock coat, a grey silk waistcoat and a shiny white clerical collar and cuffs. He slicked his hair down over his forehead in a peak and, putting his hand into his coat, stood to attention.

'Who do I look like?'

We had no answers.

'Napoleon, of course! Don't you know your history?'

'Come on, Bertie,' Mother called, 'stop teasing them.'

They went off in the car in high good humour. I was so glad Father could drive now. It was so much more elegant for Mother in her gorgeous dress. But his driving lessons had a been a great trial to Mother.

The yard at the back of the house was big and wide but when Father was teaching himself to drive he bumped into everything in it: the meat safe, the dog's kennel, the pump – and every time he let forth strings of explosive epithets.

'Damn!' he roared as his back bumper crumpled, and 'Blast!' when the front lights crashed to the ground. The man from Bushmills who came to show Father the rudiments of driving said it had been the most colourful experience of his life. Mother brought us all in out of the way of both danger and strong language.

'Daddy,' I queried later, 'why do you swear?'

'I don't swear,' he answered indignantly. 'I use descriptive and expressive words for situations where they are appropriate. Far be it from me to foul the English language. I was brought up in a city where the best is spoken. Dublin is renowned for the appropriate word. No, child, I do not swear. I have too great a love for language to dirty it. Remember that.'

I loved the way Father talked to me; the flow of words permeated my soul. I collected a library of long, impressive-sounding words and hoarded them for special occasions, often using them in the wrong context.

'A regular little Mrs Malaprop,' I heard remarked more than once.

I worried about Father's concern over money, which could be a source of conflict between us at times. He was frequently quoting Mr Micawber about having a penny to spare with the result happiness, and a penny overspent would result in us all going to the poorhouse. If we did any damage about the place, or broke anything, he said we were hastening the day when we all went to the poorhouse, or workhouse as it was called. On one of our few visits to Belfast he showed us the place, on the site of the later City Hospital. It made me shiver, so bleak and grey it looked. The image of the change in our circumstances became so clear to me that I secretly packed a trunk to take with us and hoarded up any pennies I had. Philly brought her precious things too, and we kept adding to it, against the terrible time.

Another brush with Father occurred over our names.

'Why did you call me Vivien, Daddy? It's a boy's name!' I declared indignantly.

'It is both,' Father said, '"Vivien" is the female spelling, "Vivian" the male. Your Uncle Vivian was very pleased.'

'Well, I don't like it, nor Uncle Vivian. He never speaks to us, just looks at us.' I was rebellious.

'He's a bachelor, not used to children. He's got a pot of gold and a grand house in Dalkey. You be nice to him,' he added with a twinkle in his eye.

I complained to Mother.

'I wanted to call you Veronica,' she said; 'the bushes all around the house were so pretty when you were born, all lavender and purple. But your father said it would be inappropriate for a Protestant clergyman to call his daughter Veronica.

'Well,' I decided, 'I like it. I'm going to be Veronica from today.' But I came home from school the next day and confronted Mother and Father.

'Veronica's the name of a Catholic saint,' I announced in aggrieved tones.

Father looked at me impatiently.

'I'm hardly likely to call you after a saint of any kind, now am I?' He dismissed the subject. 'You can change your name by deed poll when you are grown up.'

Philippa objected to her name too, though we always called her Phil or Philly.

Father looked at me in disgust.

'So you've got her at it too. Philippa is a grand name, Greek,' he said to her; 'be proud of it. You are lucky

73

not to be a pair of orphans, with no names at all.'

'The French teacher says I can add another "ne" to Vivien, and it will look feminine and French. I think I'll do that.'

As I went off to tell the others playing in the daisy field I heard my parents remark, 'She's full of airs and graces, that one,' and laugh together.

Father loved to tell ghost stories and he had a wicked sense of fun. He told us that when he and his brother, our Uncle Vivian, had been boys in Dublin they had, along with some pals, stuck lighted candles on the backs of crabs and let them loose in a Blackrock graveyard; the locals had thought that it was Judgement Day.

He told us the story that belongs to every county in Ireland about the woman who was buried with her rings on and when the grave robbers tried to cut them off she woke up. He told us such horrific tales that our eyes were out on our cheeks as big as saucers like the dog in the Tinder Box and Mother chided him for frightening the wits out of us. But we loved being scared sitting around and on his knees in the big chair in his cosy study, the curtains drawn and a big log fire roaring up the chimney.

The only Irish history I learned then was what he taught, or told me. He had been a young clergyman during the Rebellion in 1916. He read Sean O'Casey's plays to us with great dramatic emphasis, and was always quoting from them. The words 'murdering hate' sank into my soul. I asked him what he had done during the Rebellion.

'Sure I hid under my bed,' he replied to my eagerness, waiting on some of the drama he had engendered in me.

'You did not,' I wailed, 'and you a clergyman!'

'Stop teasing her,' ordered Mother.

'Well,' he conceded, 'I was often sent for, to comfort the dying, say a prayer over them. People were falling in the streets.'

'But weren't they Catholics?' I queried.

'Indeed I couldn't be sure what they were. And in their extremity would they be caring? Mind you, I was glad that my Latin was good.'

Father couldn't resist teasing us and telling a good story. One moonlit night when I was riding home on the crossbar of his bicycle under his coat for shelter, he pointed out a shadow going alongside us over a low hedge. When the hedge was high it disappeared, then re-appeared. I trembled with fright. The shadow was big and bulky. My hands on the handlebars inside my father's gripped tight and I urged him on. The shadow followed us up the avenue in and out of the trees, right round the house and into the yard where it lay flat when we stopped and broke up as we dismounted. I felt so foolish I was cross with Father that night.

But he went too far one night and was 'hoist with his own petard', as I heard Mother say. He had been out shooting rabbits with a bunch of local men and arrived home late with a very frightened face. Mother helped him into his favourite chair in his study beside a blazing fire and cossetted him with hot cocoa. Then she got the story out of him. On his way home he had heard a soft shoo-ing noise beside him. He had stopped and it had stopped and he had looked around and seen nothing. He had moved off again and there it had been again beside him. When he had moved fast it had gone fast ... like a train ... ch-ch-ch and when he had walked slowly it had done the same ... ch-ch-ch. The sweat had broken out all over him and he had run, the noise running with him, ch-ch-ch-ch!

Mother was mystified. It was so unlike Father to be frightened by anything.

'Sure you're just tired,' she said. 'Come on to bed now.'

He got up and moved out into the hall.

'There it is again!' he exclaimed.

Mother stood still, then: 'Walk over there,' she said.

The house was very still, all of us children in bed asleep. Father walked to the stairs, followed by the soft ch-ch-ing . Suddenly Mother burst out laughing.

'It's the leather patches on your breeches rubbing together,' she gasped. 'You never noticed it with the noises of the day around, but when it's quiet you can hear it.'

Father looked down shamefacedly at the innocent brown patches on the inside of the thighs of the cord riding breeches he wore around the countryside.

Far from curing him of telling ghost stories, he delighted ever after in telling that one against himself.

Father was likely to get us all out of our beds at an unearthly hour, as Mother described it, for special occasions. One winter a big snow was forecast by the local weather experts, farmers versed in the signs, and late one night he came rushing up the stairs and woke us all.

'Come on, come on, and see this wonderful world outside.'

Mother protested in vain but wouldn't let him take the baby. Bessie heard us and came out of her little room on the lower landing in her dressing gown. Infected by Father's enthusiasm and our excitement she rushed into the kitchen and put on her Wellington boots, threw a shovel of coal into the smouldering range, and followed us.

Outside, our sleepy eyes opened wide. The tall fir trees were like giant ladies, dressed in shining silver white. The garden shrubs had taken on the new shapes of enormous toadstools or tall thin white candles, and feathery branches glistened. The avenue was a long untrodden white carpet. With a whoop we ran down it, breaking the crackling surface with riotous delight. Father and Bessie made snowballs and threw them at us as we galloped back again. We shrieked with laughter and excitement.

The sky was a luminous dark in which a star glimmered here and there. The snowballs were flying and Mother at her bedroom window was smiling and shaking her head. Father gathered snow together and in no time a snowman stood before us. Bessie ran into the house and came out with pieces of coal for eyes and buttons, and a carrot for a nose. One of our striped scarves and a school beret dressed him beautifully.

It had begun to snow again when Mother called that we'd had enough, that we'd get our deaths of cold. Reluctantly we followed Bessie into the kitchen where the range was warm and glowing. She took a toasting fork off the wall and hooked a slice of bread on to it. She let me hold it to the red glow. We were hungry now. Mother came down to protest but Father wheedled: 'Just a little treat, to warm them up. Tomorrow is Saturday. It's Saturday now in fact.' He looked at the wall clock ticking away at half past midnight.

That big snow lasted a long time and became as deep as the hedges. The animals suffered, and some were lost, distraught farmers digging their frozen carcasses out of the ditches. Parishioners got sick and we worried when Father, carrying a shovel, had to tramp through the snow to their aid. He and the doctor often had to dig themselves out of the drifts. We couldn't go to church and once Father conducted the service for only two people, one the verger who lived close, the other Big Hugh who was afraid that he'd go back on the drink if he missed church.

When the snow began to melt there were lakes in the fields and little rivulets ran down either side of our avenue. The trees shook themselves and the sun came out. The grass was sprinkled white again, this time with daisies, and spring had broken through.

Gypsies, a Christening and Rhymers

MOTHER WAS VERY afraid of gypsies and strangers. If they came to the door she'd send Bessie, or Father would answer if he were in. They were always given food, or clothes if we had any to spare, never money.

One day we were out in the garden with Mother when she saw the gypsies coming up the road from the village. Father was away and Bessie had gone home on her day off.

'They'll be coming here,' Mother said shooing us all into the house. 'They think people who live in big houses have lots of money. Well, we haven't. Keep quiet now and maybe they'll go away.'

She locked the doors and put us in the drawing-room and even pulled the big tapestry curtains though it was daylight.

'They'll not see through them,' she whispered.

'But I want to see them,' I wailed. 'They have a lovely little house on wheels. Can I go upstairs and just peep out?'

'Well, you can, but don't let them see you.'

The gypsies stopped their caravan at the gate. It was red with a blue roof edged with wooden lace like our house had around its eaves. A horse was in the shafts, a big brown one with white patches, and another smaller one tied on at the back. A tall woman with a

brown face and black hair came up the avenue with three boys. They were very brown-skinned and black-haired and they all had bare feet, the woman too; their clothes were shabby but they were handsome. They knocked on the front door and when there was no answer they went around the house looking in at the windows. I ran to the back of the house and looked out of the bathroom window. They were in the yard. The boys went into the hen house and came out with their hands full of eggs. I wished the dogs had been there but they were out with Father who was hunting rabbits.

The woman and boys went in and out of the outhouses, then I watched in horror as the woman caught a flying hen and rung its neck then and there. She put it in her skirt, gathering it up around her booty. The boys put the eggs in. They went out of the yard and I ran to my bedroom window only to see the boys at the clothes-line stripping it of the baby clothes and the beautiful hand-worked lace christening robe, washed and whitened to be ready for the baptism ceremony on Sunday.

I raced downstairs to tell Mother.

'Mammy, Mammy, they've stolen a hen and eggs and the baby's clothes.'

Mother burst into tears and was still crying when Father returned with the dogs and several rabbits, his gun over his shoulder.

'Woman dear,' he exclaimed irritably, 'why didn't you give them something: food, apples, a turnip, anything to pacify them. They're easily pleased. At least they wouldn't have stolen right, left and centre.'

Mother continued to cry. 'Oh the dress, the beautiful dress they were all baptised in. The nighties are all I've got since the cows chewed the others.'

We'd been so sad when we had discovered that the cows in the next field had chewed several little dresses laid over the adjoining hedge right up to the bodices so that they were all green and ragged; nappies too.

'Can we afford more?' Mother sobbed.

'Indeed we can't. I'm nearly in the poorhouse as it is, what with buying the car ...'

'The robe can never be replaced, hand-made for my first baby ...' Mother ran into the kitchen still sobbing.

Father followed her. 'Come on now, stop crying,' he admonished; 'get me something to bribe them with and I'll be after them ... they'll be away towards Bushmills for the night.'

Drying her eyes with the tea-towel Mother opened a cupboard. 'Here's an apple dumpling. I made two this morning. And what about one of those rabbits?'

'Och sure, they're dab hands at trapping rabbits

themselves. Give me some of that soda bread and a pot of jam ... There, that'll do. I'll threaten them with the police for stealing my hen and the eggs ...'

Father roared away down the avenue in the Hillman car, nearly taking a gate post with him.

It seemed a long time later when he returned. We rushed out agog to know if he had got the better of the gypsies and Mother's eyes shone when he laid the bundle of baby clothes in her arms, the christening robe on top.

'It was a near thing,' he said, 'but luck was with me. When I met up with them Sergeant Stuart was just about to apprehend them himself for setting fire to a hayrick on James Clark's farm. He chased them away with the dogs instead of giving them something. They realised the game was up. I didn't even have to bribe them,' he said as he produced the apple dumpling and the bread and jam. 'I decided they'd had enough after stealing the hen and eggs.'

The baby clothes smelt of smoke and Mother had to steep them all in a bucket of Rinso suds, but they were all right and the gown was duly dried and ironed and adorned Mother's fifth child, Jean Frances, our Jenny, the following Sunday. It was a lovely ceremony and a shaft of sunlight shining through the stained glass window fell on the baby's bright hair. Then, just as Father was pouring the water on his daughter's head another stream oozed through the lace and satin of the christening gown and fell in a gleaming puddle on the baptistry floor. I was so embarrassed I stood with a red face staring at the ceiling. I gathered later that I had caused more amusement than had the baby's mishap.

Mother was still timid about callers unknown to her at the house. She didn't even like Christmas rhymers. One winter night when she was out at choir practice the rhymers arrived. We could see them through the coloured glass of the hall door, strange shapes with masked faces, carrying lanterns. We were prepared to yell with fright, but Father opened the door, let them perform and sing, and then invited them in. We all cowered behind him as he showed them into the kitchen where the range was glowing and the kettle singing on it. They removed their masks and we recognised the men and boys from the village.

'There now, children,' said Father, making tea, 'there's nothing to be afraid of. You must always look behind the mask,' he added in his Sunday voice.

We crept out from behind him and the men grinned at us and produced an assortment of sweets, a rare treat. They sang and recited again while we happily sucked aniseed balls and cinnamon lozenges, pomfret cakes and liquorice.

The King's Head

IT WAS THE yells that attracted our attention. We were grabbing our breakfast in the kitchen preparatory to the last minute dash to school when we heard them, dimmed by the distance of our avenue, yet clear enough, yells of pain.

'Merciful heavens,' my mother exclaimed, 'sounds as though someone's being murdered.'

We rushed out of the door and down the avenue to the gate. A small boy was being dragged by a girl not much bigger than himself down the hill past our house. A woman followed brandishing a branch with the leaves still on it and every yard or two the boy would break away from his sister and run to the woman with howls of anguish, clinging to her skirts. She would disentangle him and wallop him afresh. His bare legs were stained red, the socks wrinkled around the top of his boots giving no protection. He would dance like a puppet at each lashing and his bawls reached higher and higher notes.

'Merciful heavens, Mrs Taggart,' exclaimed my mother again as the woman drew abreast, 'what is wrong with the child? What has he done?'

'He won't go to school,' the woman was almost in tears herself; 'he was six last week and he has to start.'

'But ... but ...' Mother remonstrated, 'it'll never do to beat him into going. He'll never learn ... not a thing.'

The woman collapsed on to the bank beside the road and burst into tears.

'His father says he'll give him the thrashing of his life if he doesn't go.'

Just then the boy was sick, throwing up right in the middle of our gateway. Philly started to cry.

'Oh now I won't be able to go to school either. I can't bear anybody being sick. ... It makes me sick too.' She ran back up the drive, her hand over her mouth, passing Father coming down in the car.

'What is all this fuss about?' He got out of the car when he saw the little crowd. 'What's upset Philly? She looks like a ghost.'

Mother explained and Father put his arm around the small boy's shoulder, who raised eyes with rims so swollen and red in a face soaked with tears that we all choked in sympathy. He knew my father well and there was such pleading in his eyes, as to the only friend he had in the world, that Father had to swallow hard before he spoke.

'This'll never do at all, Jamie. Something is sadly wrong. It is a privilege to get an education. The master is a very good teacher. Isn't Mr Thornberry a good teacher, children?'

At the mention of the national schoolmaster's name Willie Taggart's yells began again. Father turned to his sister who was crying in the ditch with her mother.

'Come here, Polly,' Father demanded. 'Do you know why your little brother is too frightened to go to school?'

Polly hung her head.

'Bet you she's being telling him about the tortures,' Robert volunteered.

'What d'you mean?' Father asked.

'The big boys told me that Sir sticks hot needles under your nails if you can't do your sums. Bet Polly has told him.'

At this Jamie was sick again. I couldn't bear it any

longer and ran to him and hugged him hard.

'Oh Jamie, Jamie, it will be all right. Sir would never do horrible things like that to you. Sure he never uses the cane unless you are very bad. He's really a kind man and wants you to learn and grow up clever. Then when you leave national school you can come to the big school with us. Won't that be grand?'

I squeezed him to me, tears and snuffles smearing my school gymslip.

'Well, there's no school for this child today. I'll take you back up home, Mrs Taggart, and talk to his father. Polly, you go on to school and I'll see you later. You ought to be ashamed of yourself. We'll have hard work to undo the harm you have done. Come on now, children, or you'll be late too.'

We all piled into the car, my arms still around Jamie, who was shivering and whimpering like a frightened rabbit.

Jamie lived on a hill above our house called The Glass. From it there was a splendid view, away towards Portrush on the left and on a clear day the mountains of Donegal could be seen. To the right was the Giant's Causeway and the coastline sweeping right around towards Fair Head beyond Ballycastle. No one knew the origin of the name The Glass but I thought it was because the sun caught the windows of the little group of houses that sat on the skyline at the top of the hill and made them shine. More likely it came from the original Gaelic word *glas* meaning green.

Jamie's father looked up from the field he was working, and as he came towards us at Father's call I thought he was indeed a cross-looking man. But he had a regard for Father, and he belonged to the church though he never attended, and though protesting that his son couldn't be allowed to grow up a 'babby' he agreed to wait until Father called on the way back from our school to talk about it.

'Bring Jamie down to my house this evening about tea time and I'll have Mr Thornberry to meet him. Don't tell the boy now, or you'll have more trouble. Mr Thornberry is a sensible man ... he'll think of something to quiet his fears.'

Mr Thornberry was known to have unorthodox methods of teaching his pupils. He taught first mathematics with red haws and rose hips laid out on the desk in patterns. His pupils spent glowing September days searching in the hedges after school for 'counting berries'. I often envied them. It sounded an easier way to learn sums than Father's stern methods.

When Mr Thornberry arrived Father told him all about the trouble with Jamie. Then when Mr and Mrs Taggart came with Jamie, Mother had tea ready and what a tea it was! It consisted of all her own baking, things she knew a child would love: bright decorated jellies, scones and strawberry jam, currant buns, iced cake, a huge jug of ginger wine, its lovely colour glinting in the firelight. There was tea too, of course, and the rose-bud tea service was set out. Mother felt that an occasion which called for much diplomacy needed special attention.

Jamie's pale face brightened as he took his place at the table between his father and the stranger who had said 'Hello, son' and then gone on talking to the children of the house about finding field mice in the schoolroom because the corn was being cut and they running from the scythes. Jamie didn't take much notice because suddenly he felt hungry. He hadn't eaten all day since the awful sickness of the morning. I sat opposite him and winked at him once or twice to encourage him. I felt sorry for him. I could remember being scared of many things when I had been his age and even right up until my last birthday when I had reached the advanced age of ten.

Jamie, ministered to by Mother, began to relax and smile across the table. His father and mine had got into a discussion about a right of way and Trespassers Prosecuted signs, and Mr Thornberry turned to talk to Jamie.

'Now tell me, Jamie, what is it like up at The Glass? Tell me, son, what all you can see from there?'

Jamie was busy with his mouth full of currant bun, but the Master continued.

'Can you see the sea from there?'

Jamie nodded, his eyes bright.

'Isn't that the great thing? Where I live I can't see the sea at all. What else can you see from yonder? Can you see the fish in the sea, d'you know?'

Jamie shook his head.

'No, no, that'd be asking too much. But tell me now, can you see as far as the town of Portrush, son?'

Jamie's eyes lit up.

'Oh yes, oh yes,' he said enthusiastically.

'You like Portrush? And what especially do you like about Portrush?'

'Fireworks,' shouted Jamie joyfully, 'fireworks.'

'Bless my soul,' cried Mr Thornberry, 'aren't you the lucky fella to live at The Glass and get seeing the fireworks free. The rest of us have to pay to see it. Oh indeed, it's a great event, the summer fireworks in Portrush.'

At this we joined the discussion.

'We all go up to Jamie's house to see the fireworks and Mrs Taggart gives us buns and lemonade.'

'Boys-a-boys, d'you hear that! Well, I never! Now tell me, Jamie, what do you like best about the fireworks ...

the fiery fountains, the rockets, the pictures in the sky?'

He put up a hand to gently silence us bursting to tell our favourites.

'The man's head,' Jamie said at last, 'I like the man's head.'

'The head of the king. You're a great wee man, Jamie. Now tell me, what does it say under the head of the king?'

Jamie shook his head.

'Ah well, you're too young to know what it says under the picture of the king. Now these children know what it says, don't you children?'

Our enthusiastic chorus convinced him: 'God Save the King.'

'Well now, Jamie, wouldn't you like to be able to read the words in the sky under that lovely picture of the king?'

Jamie nodded.

'You'd have to go to school to learn your letters first, of course. Then you'd be able to spell out what it says.'

We waited breathlessly. I could see my mother and Jamie's mother anxiously pretending not to listen.

'Will you come to school, Jamie?' He put his hand on the boy's shoulder and continued gently: 'You come to my school, Jamie, and I'll teach you to read those words shining in the sky over Portrush by the very next fireworks display.'

Jamie stared. I nervously pushed a plate of chocolate cake close to his hand. Slowly a smile broke over his face and he nodded. Mr Taggart had to leave the room suddenly and Mother poured out a glass of ginger wine and went on pouring till it ran all over the tablecloth.

'Good lad,' said Mr Thornberry and pressed the boy's shoulder hard.

Later when they were all taking their leave in great

good spirits and my mother and Mrs Taggart had dried their eyes in the kitchen, Jamie turned back from the door and went up to Mr Thornberry.

'Will you ...' he began hesitatingly, 'will you come ... to The Glass, to see the fireworks too ... Sir?'

Mr Thornberry took Jamie's hand and shook it.

'Thank you kindly, Jamie,' he answered. 'I'll look forward to that.'

Red Herrings

THE WINTER HAD been so cold and stormy that the water froze in the yard pump and several tall trees fell in the avenue. Rathlin Island was cloaked in a thick white veil, rarely seen except for her two red eyes north and south. The moan of her fog horn was ever-present. But when spring came the levelled tree stumps made nice seats and the daffodils grew up around them. Rathlin lay peacefully prone in the width of blue Atlantic beyond the rectory and its surrounding fields.

We four children, myself, my sisters Philippa and Helen, and Robert the youngest, were out all day roaming the fields and lanes at will, bringing the first primroses and violets to Mother. She was ill again and the winter had been hard on her, Father told us. He also told us that she was expecting another baby, so she needed a lot of extra care and attention. Privately I thought that there were enough of us, but Robert hoped for a brother. Father and Bessie, our dearly loved live-in maid, were looking after Mother and hadn't much time for us. But we understood. Her illness was the only cloud on our horizon.

'Will she die of the scourge?' Helen's voice was piteous.

'No, no!' Philippa almost screamed, 'she has a fever, ru-rum-itis fever. It doesn't make you die.'

'Rheumatic fever,' I helped her out. 'Father told me. It takes a lot out of her. That's why she's so tired all the time. We have to take care of her. So long as we take great care of her she'll get well, she will, she will.'

One worrying day the doctor had been sent for and had come and gone; we were all clustered at the top of the avenue, a forlorn little heap. Father saw us from Mother's bedroom window and waved to us. Later we saw him get the car out and drive to the village. When he came back we were having tea in the kitchen. He had a kitten in his arms, a grey-striped fluffy tabby with big eyes and long inquiring whiskers. Our delight was immediate. We left our tea to follow where the kitten led, to pick him up and cuddle him, to exclaim about his beauty.

'It is a he, isn't it?'

'What'll we call him?'

'We'll ask Daddy what to call him.'

'He looks like a wee divil of a fella I once knew in Dublin. Malachy was his name. Call him Malachy. He looks like another wee divil.'

'Another cat!' Mother exclaimed when she saw the new addition. She was downstairs in her flowered dressing gown and wrapped in shawls, sitting in the window of the drawing-room overlooking Rathlin.

'Another won't matter. The other cats are wild, barn cats. They can try taming this one. They weren't getting much attention while you were so ill, my pet. It will keep them occupied,' Father reassured her.

'Poor little things, that's true,' Mother smiled sadly.

Taming Malachy wasn't easy. He was already half wild, but he was the centre of our attention. Fresh fish, chickens and rabbits, country butter and goat's milk he shared with us and he grew and thrived.

It was just at this time that Father let two old men, Jamsie Megaw and his cousin from Cork, set up a 'kipperin' business' in a disused lime kiln situated across the fields, near the cliffs, part of the rectory lands, which reached to the edge of the sea. 'Our Kingdom' we were wont to call that lovely enchanted place.

'They'll be up to no good,' Mother said when she heard of Father's altruism in offering the improbable 'entrepreneurs' the means of making an 'honest living'.

'That Jamsie Megaw has weasel's eyes,' she declared. 'I don't trust him, nor his cousin from Cork.'

'They're going to sell me fresh kippers every Friday. Jamsie comes from your own County Wicklow,' Father wheedled her.

'No better than a tinker so,' Mother was adamant.

But the kippers duly arrived at the kitchen door every Friday.

The old kiln attracted us; after all, we saw few strangers in those parts. But the occupants would not invite us in. It seemed warm and cosy in there with the door shut against the wind from the sea. They came and went in a rickety cart drawn by an ancient, very cross pony with huge yellow teeth. He was always tethered close to the kiln so that we could go no further than he allowed.

Then Malachy became sick, very sick. We were worried. We had lost pets before, favourite hens and chickens taken away by foxes or killed to make soup; a dog that had to be put down for biting the parishioners; cats that ate poison meant for rats.

'The vet'll put him away kindly for you for half a crown,' Father said. 'Better than letting him suffer.'

He produced the half crown.

We looked at it.

'Felt like Judas, I did,' I heard him say to Mother.

The doctor came to see Mother. Knowing him well, we waylaid him in the hall.

'He's eaten something that's bad for him,' the doctor

said, prodding a protesting Malachy. 'Get some oil into him, keep him warm. Then ... we'll see ... we'll see ...'

He looked at Malachy doubtfully, striking a chill into our hearts.

Father helped with the oil, warmed by Bessie on the big coal range in the kitchen.

'Stroke his tummy,' Bessie advised, 'get the oil well down.'

But Malachy lay, eyes closed, inert, in a shoe box.

That night I decided to stay awake and pray. I couldn't sleep anyway, so anxious was I about Mother first and then Malachy.

I heard Father come out of their bedroom and I got up from my knees. The weather had been mild, full of spring sunshine, but I shivered.

Father went into Robert's room, whose turn it was to watch over Malachy. Robert was lying fast asleep on the floor, the eiderdown pulled off his bed, with his arm around the shoe box in which Malachy lay. As I stood in my bedroom door Father went back to Mother. I followed and saw him wrap her in her flowered dressing gown and shawl and carry her to Robert's room.

'Come and see this,' he whispered.

They stood in the open doorway looking at the sleeping Robert.

'Such care and attention as that cat has got,' Father whispered, 'it'll be the ungrateful animal if it doesn't recover.'

They turned to go back to the bedroom and then saw me.

'I've been praying all night,' I answered their queries tearfully but not without a hint of self-righteousness.

'Come in here,' Mother urged from Father's shoulder. She stretched out her hand.

Safely in bed beside her I snuggled down. Dawn was

breaking and birds were beginning to sing. I was sleepy. Father put his hand on my head.

'The good Lord doesn't ask you to stay up all night to pray, little one; ask Him once and then trust Him.'

I fell asleep.

Next day Mother was better, able to eat breakfast, but Malachy was still inert, breathing quickly and shallowly, a pathetic little bundle. We crowded round the shoe box.

'I know what'll cure him,' Helen suddenly announced. We all looked at her in amazement. Usually diffident, she sounded suddenly assured.

'Communion wine! You know Daddy takes it to the sick. It makes them better ... or they go to Heaven,' she added, lapsing for a moment from her unwonted confidence.

We scrambled up from the floor and, carefully carrying the shoe box, went to Father's study.

'Far be it from me to begrudge the poor creature a drop of Communion wine, but I haven't any.' At the sight of our crestfallen looks he continued, 'It is ordered for Easter. We'll try it then.'

But Easter was a week away. We were disconsolate.

Then Robert had an idea.

'What about the old men in the kiln? They always smell of wine. Maybe they'll have some.'

We tore off in high excitement over the fields. Thankfully the cross pony wasn't there, nor the cart, but the door was locked and barred. Undeterred, we went around the back where there was a small opening in the stonework that acted as a chimney. It was easy to remove enough loose stones to let Robert squeeze in. Two tense minutes later he climbed back with a full bottle of pale liquid.

'It's not red, like Communion wine,' I protested.

Robert went back, them emerged again.

'It's all the same,' he said.

'Oh well, it'll do. It'll have to. Come on.'

We raced for the house and the big barn where we had left Malachy in the straw. Father was out parochial visiting and Bessie was with Mother and couldn't be disturbed.

We got Malachy's mouth open with difficulty and a great many scratches in spite of his weak state. He had strength enough to wriggle like an eel, but Philippa managed to pour a tablespoonful of the liquid down his throat despite his protests. We let go and stood back. Malachy shook his head several times, spluttered and coughed, stood up shakily, and suddenly made a dart for the barn door. We watched him go with radiant faces.

Later we sat on the wall at the end of the avenue to wait for Father's return and our accustomed ride up the avenue between the tall firs and the laburnum trees, the lumps of daffodils and drifts of bluebells.

'Hop in,' he said as the car turned in at the gate. We were breathless with our news.

'The Communion wine saved him,' we announced.

'It was my idea,' Helen insisted in spite of her diffidence.

'But ... but,' Father interrupted, 'I told you we had no Communion wine. It will arrive in time for Easter. In the meantime there isn't a drop in the house.'

'But there's lots!' Robert cried. 'In the old kiln! I saw it! Bottles and bottles of it!'

'It's true,' I said; 'it isn't a red colour but it must be good ... why ... what's the matter?'

Father brought the car to an abrupt stop. His face had paled.

'Hold on now, tell the truth now,' he urged. 'You

mean to say you got this so-called wine in the old kiln?
Did the old men give it to you? How did you get in?'

He sounded stern. We hung our heads.

'We made the hole bigger,' Robert confessed, 'so's I
could get in. We only took one bottle, only a wee taste
out of it,' he pleaded. 'We'll put it back now. Malachy is
well.'

'Listen to me.' Father was careful with his inquiries.
'Are there many bottles there?'

'Lots,' Robert assured him.

'No fish?' Father queried hopefully.

'I didn't see any. There wasn't a smell of fish, only
wine,' Robert hastened to assure him.

'Well ... well,' said Father with a deep sigh.

'I told you so!' Mother declared. 'Oh, the audacity of
them! You'd better call Constable McCann.'

'And have it all over the parish that I allowed a still
and the making of poteen to be set up on church
lands. I'd be unfrocked. Bessie, will you help me? And
you children, come on. We'd better hurry.'

We followed Father and Bessie at a fast trot to the old
kiln. Father unlocked it with his duplicate key.

'To think of my being duped like that,' he muttered
sadly and angrily, as he surveyed the bottles arranged
in neat rows and all the trappings of a poteen still set
up in the middle of the floor.

'Quick, before the light fades.' He filled his arms with
the bottles, Bessie did the same and we took two each
and followed them to the cliff edge. Father threw his
armful into the sea below, then took Bessie's and ours
and did the same.

Four trips more and the bottles were all washed out
to sea or broken on the shingle below.

When Jamsie Megaw and his cousin from Cork reappeared in their cart, less than sober after their 'business' in the town, they pulled up short. Standing at the open kiln door was Father with his shotgun. They knew him well for a crack shot in the countryside; farmers in the neighbourhood who were invaded by rabbits or foxes or pestilent crows often sent for him.

'We've been rumbled,' shouted the cousin from Cork.

'And I've been had,' shouted back Father, as he levelled the gun.

The cross pony suddenly took fright and reared, almost tumbling the rascally pair out of their cart, then turned and bolted, back across the field, bouncing the cart like a ball, reached the road and fled.

'That'll be the last of them,' Father said, lowering his gun.

'You wouldn't really have shot them, Father?' I emerged from the kiln anxiously.

'Of course not.' Father was recovering from his chagrin. 'I've too much respect for that ould nag of theirs. I hope it leads them a rare dance!'

The next morning the milkman rang the door bell for his week's money. I answered the door and when Father came the milkman handed him a packet of kippers.

'The old men in the kiln had an order in with my brother the fishman for these kippers every Friday,' he explained, 'but they're not there and the place is shut up.'

'They'll not be back,' Father said sadly. 'Your brother may continue the order, good kippers they were. How much do I owe you?'

The milkman named a sum.

'Made a shillin' out of me they did, the divils,' Father murmured with a wry grimace.

As he went to close the door his eyes lit up.

'Children, children,' he called, 'here's somebody to see you.'

We all ran to where he was pointing. There in the sunshine, sitting on one of Mother's ornamental stone pedestals, was Malachy. He blinked at us – or did he wink? – and serenely began to clean his fur.

Snowberries
and Castor Oil

WE WERE WARNED about eating berries that could be poisonous, and after seeing one of Father's pet goats die in agony from eating laburnum pods we were very careful. But we often sucked 'guzzoms' as we called sorrel – small dark green leaves that grew amongst grass, tasted lemony, and were very thirst quenching. Mother said they gave us worms.

Father engaged an old man called Jimmy to cut hedges and do general jobs about the place. He wore an ancient black frock-coat and we teased him unmercifully by swinging on the tails. Standing on a bank clutching the hedge with two of us on his coat tails was no mean feat. He got his own back and electrified us by eating worms. He put them in his pocket and drew them out one by one when we were watching him, goggle-eyed, and dropped them into his mouth.

One day when Mother had made him a good dinner with a pudding and a slice of cake we gathered in the kitchen while he ate. He emptied the pudding and the cake on to his big plate of meat and vegetables and mashed up the lot, washing it all down with a glass of buttermilk. Mother chided us for 'gawking' at the poor man while he ate. But he, with a twinkle in his eye, drew out a long, still wriggling worm from his pocket and ate that too.

We were playing at being gypsies, stimulated by their recent visit, and we made up a fire in a corner of the apple orchard. But how to light it: we tried a piece of glass and the sun. Robert had heard about how to do it, but it didn't work because the sun kept going behind a cloud. So I slipped into the kitchen while no one was about and found I could just reach the shelf over the range by standing on a chair and feeling along it to where I knew the matches were kept. I also took some sugar and milk and one of the oldest saucepans. I had decided that we would make toffee.

The fire lit very well and we put the sugar and milk on to boil. It went on boiling until it boiled over and nearly put our fire out. We added some water.

'This is not going to turn into toffee,' I said, disappointed. 'There is hardly any left.'

'Put some of these in,' Robert suggested, holding out a handful of white berries. Then he went to the snowberry hedge and got more. We tasted the mixture: it was sweet and sticky and nice, so we ate the lot.

The pains began soon after the fire died.

'I'm going to be sick,' wailed Helen, and she was. Then Robert was sick, and both of them ran yelling for Mother.

Phil and I sat beside the ashes of the fire holding our stomachs. The pains were awful and when Mother saw our white faces she put us to bed and as soon as Father came from parish visiting she sent him off for the doctor. When they arrived the doctor had a consultation in the hall with Mother. Then they came upstairs to where Phil and I were in bed feeling very sorry for ourselves. Helen and Robert had been violently sick several times and were now recovering in the kitchen with Bessie fussing over them. But we hadn't been sick and Mother said that was why the pains were so bad. The doctor felt our sore tummies and looked very solemn.

'Your father is coming to help me,' he said, as Father came through the door brandishing his bicycle pump.

'Which end, Doc?' he roared.

We wailed in apprehension. Mother and Bessie appeared at the door shaking their heads.

'We'll try this first,' said the doctor holding up a bottle of castor oil, 'half a bottle each.'

'Oh God!' burst out Phil.

Father brandished the bicycle pump.

We downed the castor oil and vowed never to eat snowberries again.

Another mishap occurred when we buried Robert. We decided to play at funerals and as the big lawn had been cut there was a huge pile of fresh grass cuttings. We made Robert lie down, shut his eyes and cross his hands on his chest. He was used to obeying us and lay down without any objections. Then we shovelled the grass cuttings on to him and smoothed them down, stuck some flowers into the mound and stood around singing hymns. Just as I had climbed on to the improvised pulpit of a garden seat and was loudly declaiming the funeral oration, as I had heard Father do, he arrived across the lawn.

'Who's dead?' he inquired, and at a chorus of 'Robert', hurriedly and with many descriptive exclamations such as 'you pack of she-devils', excavated Robert, who was spluttering and gasping and spitting grass. Visibly shaken, Father forbade us ever to play that game again.

'Apart from the danger to Robert you were making a mockery of God's holy ordinances.'

Whatever that meant, it sounded a terrible sin and we were suitably chastened.

When Robert was able to play games with us we dressed him up in one of Helen's little dresses.

'You be a girl,' we admonished him; 'this is a girl's game. We are all at a girls' boarding school.'

I had been reading stories of such tales as *The Fifth Form at Mallory Towers* and *The Worst Girl in the School*, and nothing short of acting out the plots and intrigues could satisfy my longing to be part of such exciting establishments.

'Robert ... you'd better be Roberta,' I decided, and he obligingly divested himself of his shorts and jersey and donned a frilly dress with panties to match. I added a bow to his hair. Mother looked in on us as we played in Phil's and my big bedroom overlooking the apple trees and cabbage roses in the kitchen garden. We had re-arranged the bedclothes in lines on the floor to represent a dormitory. She saw her son standing there resplendent in frills, and a slight frown replaced her smile. She left to go downstairs and a little later we were summoned to the study.

Father looked sternly at us as we stood in a row, Robert in the middle. There was an unnerving silence. I began to feel foolish again but I didn't know why. I watched a sort of twitch at the corner of my father's mouth. Now he folded his hands across the waistcoat and intertwined his fingers in the chair, slowly. I felt I'd have to go to the lavatory and crossed my legs tightly. Phil began to giggle nervously. Mother looked in and, observing the situation, she whispered my father's name pleadingly, then retreated.

Still interlocking his fingers with the chain he said sternly. 'I had three daughters and a son. Where is he?'

We pushed Robert forward hurriedly.

'Whose damn fool idea was this?' Father suddenly exploded and turned his head away.

'Mine,' I shivered, my legs still tightly crossed. 'We were playing girls' school.'

There was another silence. Father's shoulders seemed to be shaking. He swivelled round suddenly again.

'There is male and there is female,' he began. I thought he was going to preach us his Sunday's sermon and wondered how I'd last out.

'You three, my daughters,' continued Father, 'are female. Your brother is a male. You must understand that there is this fundamental division of the human race ...' He paused, blew his nose loudly and lengthily, making his eyes red with the effort.

Suddenly he looked sternly at us again. 'Take this boy and put his trousers back on him!'

We grabbed Robert's hands and prepared to run.

'And learn to respect him,' Father thundered after us as we reached the stairs.

Mother came out of the kitchen and flew into the study slamming the door behind her, and as I raced for the top landing and the lavatory I heard them laughing their heads off far below.

Story-telling, Ghosts and Ghouls

WHEN JANE CAME to mind us while our parents were out she told us wonderful stories. Unmarried though she was, she was a real romantic. She told us of the giant Finn McCool building the causeway to get over to his giantess sweetheart in Scotland.

'Daddy says he was going to fight another giant!' we protested.

'Your daddy's a fine man,' she said solemnly, 'but he's from the south. How would he know about Finn McCool and his sweetheart in these northern parts!'

'What was her name?' we queried.

'Flora, Flora MacDonald,' she continued. 'Finn could see her on a clear day waving to him from the coast of Scotland.'

'Was that the same Flora that saved Bonnie Prince Charlie?' I asked doubtfully. I was learning history.

'Could be, I've no doubt,' Jane replied dreamily. 'She was that sort of girl.'

'What happened to them?' we cried together.

'He was so impatient to take her in his arms and she to be in them that they couldn't wait for the causeway to be finished and they plunged into the raging sea of Moyle to be together and were drowned.'

We burst into the comfort of tears.

'Tell us another,' we chorused.

'Dunluce Castle now, there's a tale,' continued Jane after drying her eyes and ours.

'The Lady of the Castle was giving a great banquet one night. She loved parties, Lady Antrim. You can imagine the scene,' her eyes shone as bright as ours, 'the walls hung with lovely embroidered tapestries, gold and silver goblets on the long tables, gold-edged plates and cutlery, ladies and gentlemen in beautiful clothes, everything of the best. She was a Duchess before she married the Earl of Antrim and so she knew how to do things in the best tradition.'

'Was it not cold there?' I asked, knowing only the ruin with the sea pounding below.

'No, no,' continued Jane, 'there were huge fireplaces in the walls piled high with logs and brick ovens in the kitchen where the cooking for the feast was going on ...' she paused. '... Oh ... oh, the kitchen ...'

We waited breathlessly in spite of having heard the story many times.

'Suddenly in the midst of all the music and laughter in the dining-room there was a terrible sound, a roar, a crashing and rumbling like thunder and the kitchen and all the servants were sucked into the sea and drowned.'

After a suitable dramatic pause Jane went on. 'There was a tinker man sitting in an alcove in the passage to the kitchen mending pots. He was in love with one of the maids, Maeve her name was. He suddenly looked down into a drop of one hundred feet and saw his love tossed into the cauldron of the angry sea and lost forever.'

Our tears began to fall again. Jane held up her hand.

'Lady Antrim wouldn't stay in Dunluce another night after that. But the tinker man comes back, looking for his lost love, and sings a lament. You can hear it if you

are passing Dunluce on stormy nights.'

I vowed that that was one thing I would never do.

'Tell us more, Jane,' we begged.

'Did you ever hear of Turlough of Dunseverick? Well, there's only a bit of the castle left but once that was a great castle like Dunluce. And long, long ago the north coast was invaded by the Norsemen, big fierce men who wore clothes of fur and skins, and helmets with huge horns curling up, and shining shields and swords. They captured Dunseverick Castle and one of them fell in love with the beautiful daughter of the house, Catriona O'Cahan. He forced her to marry him, but in the middle of the ceremony her brother Turlough came back from battles abroad and killed the Dane. Then the other Danes killed Turlough and Catriona was so grief stricken she threw herself from the castle window into the sea!'

'Don't tell me there was more wailing on stormy nights!' I said in precocious tones, and Helen whispered, 'It's very sad up here.'

'Tell us a happy ending one,' demanded Phil.

'Oh indeed I will,' Jane smiled and put some more turf on the fire. 'I'll tell you Rathlin Boy. There was once a little boy lived on Rathlin Island who was daft enough to try to climb a fairy thorn tree.'

'What happened to him?' we shivered in anticipation.

'He disappeared! His poor mother was distracted. His father and brothers searched the island. The islanders said he must have fallen over the cliffs, after bird's eggs maybe. But no body was found. Then his clothes were found, a small forlorn heap. Everybody shook their heads.

'"The fairies will have taken him. I saw him near the fairy thorn," an island boy volunteered.

'Everybody knew that when the fairies steal a human child they wash him to clear him of every trace of his human life and throw away his clothes. Then they dress him in green and make him their own. How his mother grieved!

'But after a while she began to believe she'd see him again and after one year she was down by the shore gathering dulse when she saw him. She called to him, "Shane, Shane, come to me!" He ran to her and clung to her.

'"I thought I'd never see you again, Mammy!"

'She held him from her to look at his green clothes. How, she wondered, did he get away. Then she noticed he had a sore and swollen finger.

'"Come home, my darlin'," she said, and she led him away quickly, looking back frequently for fear of the fairies.

'When she had him safely home she bathed him and

STORY-TELLING, GHOSTS AND GHOULS

put on his own clothes which she had kept washed
and clean. Then she bathed the finger and out came a
long thorn. She held it up.

'"They didn't wash that away, and it has saved you, a
thorn from the fairy tree."

'Shane couldn't remember his year with the fairies,
but the boys at school called him "fairy boy" until he
was big enough to punch them for it. He never inter-
fered with a fairy thorn tree after that.'

'Well, thank goodness,' we yawned, 'there's no wailing
out at sea in that story.'

'You'd better be off to your beds,' Jane declared, 'or
I'll be in trouble. Goodnight now and don't be having
any bad dreams.'

'Goodnight, dear Jane,' we hugged her. 'Thank you
for the stories.'

'You're welcome,' she smiled.

Father left her home to her cottage in the village. She
couldn't go herself for fear of all the sad ghosts she'd
conjured up to haunt her.

Another story Jane told us was about the Brown Bull
of Cooley. 'The biggest bull in Ireland,' she began, 'and
it belonged to Queen Maeve of Connaught.'

'Did we really have an Irish queen?' I was suddenly
excited, 'like the kings and queens of England?'

'Oh, there were indeed kings and queens here, but a
long long time ago. There were four kingdoms you see
...'

'I know, I know,' I interrupted; 'Ulster, Munster,
Leinster and Connacht!'

'That's right,' Jane continued, 'and there was always
great rivalry between them, and boastfulness. But the
greatest boaster of them all was Queen Maeve of
Connacht!'

'What was she like? Was she beautiful? Did she wear a crown?'

'She was tall and very handsome, with honey-coloured hair. She always dressed in green velvet lined with red satin, and wore a golden band round her fore-head, and when she led her troops into battle she used to dye her hair russet red, red as the lining of her dress, some said with blood, but more likely with the juice of hawthorn berries.

'But she was a terrible boaster,' Jane continued. 'She even argued with her husband! They were both rich and owned great herds of cattle and sheep and she loved to say "mine is the best" or "mine is the biggest", just like I hear you children do many a time ...'

'So she owned the biggest bull,' I interjected to change the subject.

'Oh indeed, the Brown Bull of Cooley was a terrible big bull. You never go into a field where there's a bull, children, don't you know that?'

We nodded fervently.

'Well, Queen Maeve boasted so much about her big bull that it came to the ears of the King of Ulster, Conor. He decided he'd like to see it and maybe ...' Jane hesitated and chose her words carefully, 'maybe it would get together with one of his best cows and then she would have just such a bull in nature's good time and he, Conor, could boast as hard as Maeve. But Maeve knew what he was after and she got a wise woman to make up a special drink of herbs for her bull so that he wouldn't go near to Conor's cows. Then she sent the bull into Ulster and it rampaged all over the country and couldn't be caught. Conor was very angry for it caused great damage and frightened the people out of their wits. At last King Conor's spearmen man-aged to corner the Brown Bull and with many wounds

114

inflicted on it, it roared loudly and turned back the way it had come and stampeded off at a great pace into Connacht.'

'Was it never seen again?' we queried.

'Oh, well now, I don't know,' said Jane, 'there's those as say it is still rampaging through Ulster, causing mayhem and trouble all the way. Maybe it's only its ghost.'

But a wee while later we awoke one morning very early to a great sound of stamping and shouting in the corner of the field next to ours. It was ours too but was let to a farmer who was one of father's parishioners. We looked out of the bedroom window. There were a lot of men shouting and laughing and raising their voices: 'Hup there, ye boy ye, hup there,' and 'Come on, ye girl ye, that's the lady, that's the girl!'

We hurried downstairs.

'It must be the Brown Bull of Cooley!' we exclaimed as we raced out into the daisy field and saw a big brown bull and a small brown cow in the corner beyond the hedge. The bull was on a long rope held by a young fellow who looked very scared and stood half way up the field. The other men held sticks and switches out of the hedge.

Suddenly they saw us and one of them who knew us came forward and said in a kindly, shy sort of way, 'Now look, wee lasses, this is not a sight for young eyes. Go on back to the house now, like good weans.'

'Is it the Brown Bull of Cooley,' I asked fearfully, 'rampaging through Ulster?'

'Well I don't know about that now, but it is Tom McCahan's bull all right and the wee cow is mine.' He looked anxiously towards the house.

'Now go on childer or his Reverence will have something to say ...'

Just then Bessie came running.

'Come on outa that you lot, watchin' that filthiness! Haven't I told you often that curiosity killed the cat!'

She addressed the men. 'You might have gone to the back end of the field to get on with your dirty business!'

She hustled us away up the daisy field and indoors without any answers and our curiosity unsatisfied.

Later I tackled my father in the study. He roared laughing when I told him the story of the Brown Bull of Cooley.

'That Jane's imagination is running away with her.'

'Bessie says what they were doing in the field is filthy.'

He looked at me and closed his book with his finger in it.

'Not filthy, child; earthy, of the earth, earthy. Nature is wonderful, but not all of her activities are beautiful, some are downright ugly. But you like the little calves, don't you?'

I nodded, hoping for more information, but Father only said, 'Well then, cows and bulls are the fathers and mothers of the calves.'

'But how?' I wanted to ask.

'That'll do you now. You can't learn everything all at once. And don't go near the men with the bull and the cow. You'll only embarrass them, and a bull is dangerous at the best of times, and doubly so when he's excited.'

He saw my anxious look.

'The little cow will come to no harm.'

He opened his book again and I had to be content.

Life was full of a mysterious quality for me. I was curious about many things and never could get all the answers I wanted. Interesting conversations would

116

stop when I came near and I often heard them say: 'Big
Ears is listening.'

One such occasion occurred when I heard Mother
telling Bessie and Katie in the kitchen that she was
going to have another baby.

'My fifth!' she complained plaintively, 'I get pregnant
at the drop of a hat!'

As she went through the kitchen door I heard Katie
say solemnly to Bessie: 'Och the poor dear, it's not a
hat that's been dropped!' They both burst out laughing
and then saw me. I ran before they could call me Big
Ears again.

The story of the Brown Bull of Cooley still held unan-
swered questions, and as soon as I could I returned to
it again.

'Did King Conor have a Queen?' I asked Jane.

'He was a young man when a baby girl was born to
the wife of a friend of his and he was told that this
child would be so beautiful there would be nothing but
fighting over her. So, to avoid this trouble, he sent her
away to a hidden part of the country to be fostered and
reared until she grew up and then he would make her
his wife and that would prevent any of the trouble fore-
told.

So she grew up with kindly foster parents and an old
nurse to see that nobody came near her and that she
was kept for the king. She grew like a wild flower, very
beautiful indeed. Her name was Deirdre.'

'What was she like?' I urged eagerly.

'She was as slender as a fairy, with hair like moonlight and grey-green eyes. Some said she was like a
snowdrop, others a primrose. But she was strong-
minded, some might say wayward. When she was seventeen years old she saw in the distance a beautiful
young man riding one of the king's horses. He was as

117

dark as she was fair, and he wore a green cloak edged with silver braid. She ran to her nurse, "Get him for me, find him for me," she demanded.

"'But you are promised to the king!" the old woman protested.

"'I shall throw myself into the lake if you don't get him for me," Deirdre screamed.

"'What shall I tell the king?" The old lady was trembling.

"'Don't tell him anything, just go to the court, now, right now, and find out who the young man is who wears a green cloak with a silver edge. Go on, so that he is still wearing it. I want only him. Find his name. Go!"

The old woman went, grumbling about spoilt children, but Deirdre stood still and pointed towards the far blue hills.

"'Hurry," she called, "take the ass and cart. I'll be waiting."

'A long time later the old woman returned, exhausted.

'Deirdre ran when she saw her coming. "Well, did you find him? Who is he?"

The old woman could hardly answer she was so tired. "His name is Naisi," she gasped.

"'Did you tell him about me?" Deirdre cried.

"'I couldn't," the old woman gasped; "the king saw me and summoned me to give me this bale of white silk for your wedding dress and bid me get you ready to be his bride."

"'I won't! I can't!" wailed Deirdre, "I only want Naisi. Go back and tell him."

"'That I cannot do," the old woman climbed down from the cart. "I am too old and too tired. I will die if I have to do that journey again. Come, like a good girl, and I will plait your hair. It is all wild and tangled."

'Deirdre's tears flowed but she submitted and went indoors with her old nurse.

'When the nurse was recovered she began to unfold the white silk. She draped it over Deirdre and braided her pale gold hair into a crown high on her head. Then she showed her the mirror.

'"Look, my sweet," she cried, "look what a queen you will be!"

'"No, no," Deirdre screamed, "I will not. I want none but Naisi," and she ran to her bedroom and wept.'

'What happened? What happened?' we cried as Jane stopped for breath.

'Well, one day Deirdre, pale and sad, wandered outside and down to the lake. "Naisi, Naisi," she called and looked into the lake ready to jump. There she saw three horsemen ride up on the far side and looking up she saw it was Naisi on the leading horse.

'"Who calls?" he cried and turned his horse to ride around the lake to where Deirdre stood, the two other horsemen following.

'"I called. I am Deirdre," and she held out her arms.

'"The betrothed of the king?" Naisi cried, reining in his horse and looking down into her eyes.

'"I can never marry the king," Deirdre said. "I love you, only you."

'"And I you," Naisi answered, dismounting from his horse.'

'Gracious!' I interrupted, 'that was quick!'

'That's the way of true love,' Jane replied dreamily. 'Love at first sight.'

'What did they do?' we chorused. 'What did the king do?'

'They had to go away, to Scotland, Naisi and Deirdre and Naisi's two brothers, for they knew the king would

be terribly angry and vengeful. They stayed away for
several years and Naisi and his brothers fought for the
king of Scotland. Then one day the Scottish king saw
Deirdre and wanted her for his own. Naisi was forced
to flee again with her and his brothers to a lonely west-
ern isle. There they stayed until King Conor heard of
where they were. He sent a messenger to lure them
back to Ulster, saying he had forgiven them. She didn't
trust King Conor, but she was homesick and longed for
her own country. So they went back with the messenger. When they were brought to the king, supposedly to
a welcoming feast, they saw instead the block, still covered with blood from the last man beheaded.'

'Oh God!' exclaimed Philly.

'Now, you know you are not allowed to swear,' admonished Jane.

'I wasn't swearing,' Philly protested; 'it was a prayer.
Did the king have them all killed?'

'The three brothers knelt together and put their
heads on the block.'

We held our breath.

'No Ulsterman wanted to do the awful deed so a hired
soldier from Norway raised the axe and cut off the
three heads at once!'

We were shocked and silent.

'What happened to Deirdre?' I whispered.

'The king still wanted her for his queen, but she laid
herself down beside Naisi and, lamenting with great
sorrow, she died,'

'Oh Jane,' I exclaimed, 'what a tragedy! Is it true?'

'True? True?' Jane answered vaguely. 'How do I
know? I wasn't alive then. But it has been told, and
told again and again, until it comes to our ears, and so
it is passed on.'

'It is what is called a myth, or a legend,' Father explained when I told him the story later. 'It represents things that happened, and if it happened it happened a very long time ago. We don't chop off people's heads now, child, so don't worry. Jane is getting a bit bloodthirsty.'

And after we had a restless night of bad dreams he must have spoken to Jane, for next time she came she said, 'So you want bedtime tales! Shall I tell you "Cinderella"? "The Sleeping Beauty"?'

'No, no,' we chorused, 'those are soppy. Tell us real stories, not fairy tales.'

Jane smiled slowly and began. 'I'll tell you about the man who met the Devil!'

'How did he know it was the Devil?' We shivered.

'Sure, it was the night of the snow. The men met the stranger at the crossroads near the Giant's Causeway. He wore a long black cloak and a tall black hat. They stood and talked and the stranger told yer man how to get rich quick. Then he said goodnight and with a swirl of his cloak went away on the untrodden snow. When yer man looked down the way that the stranger had gone there in the snow was the mark of a cloven hoof!'

We looked fearfully at each other. We knew what a cloven hoof was on an animal, but to think that a person might have one!

'Now don't you dare have nightmares tonight or his Reverence will have me head in me hands!'

She was a bit huffed after Father's admonitions and refused to tell any more tales that night. But for years afterwards we would follow visitors and parishioners alike, suspiciously looking at their footprints, whenever there was snow, and a walk on the sand, always a delight, became exciting and mysterious.

Aunty May
and the Witch

WHEN WE HEARD that Aunty May and our cousin Olivia were coming to stay our joy knew no bounds. But Philly and I often had a row about who should go to Belfast in the car to meet our visitors off the Dublin train. If Uncle Harold came up on the train with them and brought his cello there would only be room for one of us in the car, the cello and the cases taking up so much space. But Uncle Harold, who ran a hotel in Kingstown and played in a little orchestral ensemble there, never knew until the last moment whether he and his cello could come or not.

The dispute was settled on this occasion by the arrival of a telegram to say that only Aunty May and Olivia were coming, so Philly and I piled into the car, full of excitement. The drive to Belfast was a hazardous journey, Father's driving being very erratic. He carried on a continuous running commentary on every aspect of the car's performance.

'Sure, she's a grand car if only her brakes will hold,' he declared as we breasted the top of a steep hill, with an added exhortation to us to say our prayers.

'I think we'll just make it now,' he said more than once, which didn't exactly fill us with confidence

On one part of the journey we passed through peat bogland between two rows of tall fir trees on either side of the road. Father told us that if it was dark on the way back we'd see the dead of long ago rising all white and shining from their graves there. We shuddered, believing him. After all, wasn't he a clergyman?

We arrived at Great Victoria Street Station in time for the Dublin train. Father eagerly scanned the arriving locomotive as the steam settled around it; he was very fond of Aunty May, who liked a joke and laughed a lot.

And there they were, Aunty Mary wearing beautiful clothes and perfume. We stared at Olivia silently, suddenly struck dumb with shyness. She wore such beautiful clothes: town clothes they were, with white socks and red, buckled shoes. She had a red coat with a velvet collar and her hands were hidden in a little white fur muff. Her reddish-brown hair, which Philly and I had always envied, was curlier than ever, and I hated my straight lanky hair and my navy school burberry as never before.

Aunty May broke the ice by hugging us all and soon we were having tea in the station buffet, a treat for us. There were buns. We never had buns at home except at the Sunday school outing or Christmas party. There were currant buns and iced buns and doughnuts, scones and a huge pot of tea.

Then a further treat was in store when we went to Woolworths. The only shop we ever saw normally was the General Store in Lisnagunogue which sold everything from acid drops and liquorice to cornmeal and cabbage, paraffin oil, calico and green soap. At Christmas it would import a few toys, Christmas stockings full of novelties and children's annuals. Woolworths bowled us over. We looked at every counter and bought Mother a little china vase for sixpence; a cloth book for baby Jenny for three pence; a toy gun for Robert and a tiny toy shop for Helen for six pence each. I bought a celluloid baby doll in a dress and shawl with my six pence and Philly chose a pretty flowered tin tea-set with hers. Then I remembered Bessie. I had two pence in my pocket which I had saved and with that I bought her a lace-edged handkerchief.

Surfeited with pleasure, we drove home through Antrim, Ballymoney and Ballymena. Aunty May sat in the front with Father and they talked and laughed all the way. It began to get dark and as we approached the tunnels of trees through the bog I remembered what Father had said about the dead. I whispered to Philly, then we both whispered to Olivia. We stared out of the car windows, three pairs of large eyes, and sure enough all over the bog there were white things, moving. The car lights illuminated them and they shone clear and bright before our eyes. Father and Aunty May were too engrossed in conversation to notice us, frozen in fascinated horror on the back seat. Soon we were through the trees and looking back we could see them no more. Later, I asked Bessie about it.

'That'll be the bog-cotton – it shines at night. You'd hardly notice it in the daytime. Pretty it is. Watch for it by moonlight – there's a sight for ye now.'

I wondered about my Father.

'Daddy said it was the dead rising,' I whispered to Aunty May later, still wondering.

'Sure, your Daddy's a great man for a yarn – all Dublin men are,' she smiled. 'But listen, ducky, wouldn't it be beautiful to rise like the bog-cotton, white and shining, all the way to Heaven, when you are dead. It's as nice a story as any. Don't worry about it, pet.'

She was so reassuring I forgot my fears, though I never travelled that road with ease afterwards.

Mother's pleasure in her sister's visit infected us all.

She wasn't always well: she was very thin and often in pain, and her poor hands were twisted by rheumatoid arthritis. Father used to try to make her drink Guinness, 'to put a bit of meat on your bones,' he'd urge, but she hated its bitter taste.

She had to spend weeks in bed sometimes and we missed her, even though we were in and out of her room like yo-yos. But when Aunty May and Olivia came all was different. Mother's pretty face shone with pleasure, the house rang with laughter and music again. Aunty May had a great contralto voice, and when visitors came and the drawing-room was full of singing we crept out of bed and ranged ourselves along the landing, our legs hanging through the banisters, listening. Once Philly couldn't resist joining in in a loud, accurate imitation of Aunty May's soulful rendering of the song 'My Task'. She gave us all away. The drawing-room door opened and Father stood in the hall and looked up at us. I couldn't make out whether he was being really cross or not, but Aunty May and the visitors quickly shut the drawing-room door and smothered their laughter behind it. We crept guiltily off to bed, but next day we held a concert of our own in the coach house and imitated them all to our heart's content. I was the pianist, racing my hands up and down a board we had painted to resemble a piano keyboard.

With Olivia, our new companion, those summer holidays took on a special quality. She discarded her buckled shoes and borrowed a pair of Wellington boots with 'gutties' for play. We invented new games, played tricks on each other, made houses in the long grass; we built a fairy grotto in the bank of the tennis lawn, tending it daily with offerings for the 'wee folk' of flowers, bits of cake, thimbles of lemonade, a sugar lump.

The sun shone and scarcely ever did Rathlin's fog horn moan. The days were warm and light until long beyond our regular bedtime. We were often allowed to stay up, it being impossible to sleep. When we did go we spent the time flying between our bedrooms, changing beds and bedfellows, shrieking with laughter or scaring each other by hiding in unexpected places and jumping out upon our victims, until sometimes it would all end in tears. Then Father would come roaring up the stairs calling us a pack of demons. Mother put us all back to bed and Aunty May brought our favourite treat – butter-balls rolled in soft brown sugar.

The windows had to be left open because of the heat, so we were awake again with the birds singing in their dawn chorus. We were allowed to read books then, quietly, so as not to wake the baby and to let Mother rest for as long as possible. When we heard Bessie leave her room on the lower landing we crept down after her in our nightgowns and she made us toast on the fire in the big range in the kitchen. It was the only means of cooking except for a paraffin stove, so the kitchen was beautifully warm in winter and suffocating in summer. Poor Bessie got very hot and red-faced, forever wiping her forehead with her apron. She opened the doors and the window where the scent of cabbage roses wafted in on the early morning breeze. The milk came in a big can, the water had to be pumped from the yard and stood in white pails covered in butter muslin in the pantry to keep cool.

One morning we came down to find a whole herd of cows in the garden eating Mother's vegetables and flowers. We rushed to chase them, Bessie at the head. Only Olivia lagged behind. She wasn't used to cows and was afraid of them. But at our yells of 'Shoo – shoo!' they turned tail and trundled off down the avenue into the road where an apologetic farmer rounded them up and drove them to their field where he hurriedly mended the fence. The havoc they left in the kitchen garden made Mother cry when she saw it.

Another early morning there was terrible chaos in the henhouse, a clucking and squawking to wake the dead. We rushed out in our night-clothes in time to see a fox race out of the henhouse with a plump hen, one of Father's prize Rhode Island Reds, in his jaws, the greedy eyes of him shining red. We raced upstairs for Father but by the time he'd jumped out of bed and into his long johns and vest and grabbed his gun from the top of the wardrobe the fox was miles away. A flapping skylight on the henhouse roof had to be mended then and there.

'He'll be back, the divil,' Father declared, 'and I'll be waiting on him.'

Sure enough, early next morning while Father waited behind the yard wall with his gun poised, the long, slinky form of the fox slid along the hedge of the rectory field, eager for another feast while still fat from the previous morning's catch, greed being a fox's middle name. As he got closer, there was a loud bang from Father's gun and he was dead.

Father lifted him by the brush and held him aloft, triumphant. We hated the fox but we couldn't look at him dead and ran to Mother. She too hated the killing that often had to be done in the country. She could never wring a chicken's neck for the pot; Father always had to do it. He closed the yard doors when this operation had to take place, and put us out, but we glued our eyes to the cracks in the door. When he chopped the heads off the chickens destined for the table, they fell off the chopping black and ran about for a few bloody seconds without their heads. No horror film ever equalled that sight for me.

The local farmers congratulated Father on his good shooting of the fox, which made up for our lack of enthusiasm.

In spite of Mother's delight in the visit of Aunty May and Olivia her health deteriorated again and she had to go to bed. Bessie called us in from whooping around the house in a wild game of Tig.

'Your poor Mam needs a bit of quiet. Will you ones take yourselves off down the fields for a while. Don't get out of sight of the house, now, so that I can see what you're at. I'll make a picnic tea for you.'

She packed lots of jam sandwiches and apples from the garden and a tin mug.

'You'll get plenty of spring water down by the stream. Don't fall in now,' she admonished as we set off.

We put all our dolls in a wicker pram and Robert

brought an old teddy bear with the stuffing falling out of it, and squeezed it in with the dolls. We put Jennie in the go-cart, a double wooden seat with shafts and big round wheels. Bessie tied her to the front seat with a dressing-gown girdle, and we put the picnic basket on the other seat. Olivia and I pushed it and Robert and Helen clutched hands and followed us.

'Where shall we go?' I asked Olivia excitedly. 'I mean, what'll we call the place?'

She knew what I meant.

'What about Mandalay, or Samarkand?' Olivia was very well read, I thought. But so was I.

'I think Timbuktu sounds great,' I replied not to be outdone. 'Aunt Lily says we might as well live there, whenever she comes here.'

'Is there a beach at Timbuktu?' Olivia asked doubt-fully. 'The children just love a beach.' The wicker pram was hung about with buckets and spades.

'Oh yes,' I said loftily, 'a beach of course, and islands and plenty of water to paddle in and rocks and pools ...'

We followed a path through some fields, being careful to shut gates behind us, and came to the stream. It was wide and shallow with spits of shingle and clear, clean running water.

'Perfect,' declared Olivia.

We took off our socks and shoes and paddled, Olivia and I taking care of Jennie who could stand but not walk yet. We held her in a shallow pool where the water just reached over her fat little feet. She promptly sat down in it and her terry nappy and woolly socks were soaked immediately. We looked at her in consternation, but as she was quite happy drinking handfuls of the clear water and soaking the rest of herself we left her to it. Olivia and Helen paddled their dolls in the stream while Robert splashed them and raised indignant yells.

'Stop that,' I ordered him. 'Boys are all the same,' I commented resignedly to Olivia in imitation adult tones.

We ate our sandwiches and apples, the six of us sitting along the bank, legs in the stream. Buttercups, bluebells, bird's-foot trefoil and daisies carpeted the margins of the stream. The sky was high and blue and white clouds had silver edges. A lark hovered and sang, bell-like. The quiet invaded our young souls and we were silent.

Suddenly the air was shattered by a shriek from Olivia. She stood like a statue, one hand clasped to her mouth, the other pointing shakily. There was her precious baby doll, one I coveted, floating downstream and heading for the deeper water that flowed under some willows and into the next field.

Robert splashed violently after it, but it swirled in an eddy suddenly and was gone. Olivia burst into a loud wail.

'Come back, Robert,' I called; 'it's too deep and that's Mad Annie's field.'

We all looked at each other. Mad Annie lived in an old farm cottage at the head of the next field. She roamed the countryside 'not right in the head', the people said, and we kept our distance.

'She is a witch,' one of the village children had told me. Father said she had lost her husband at sea and couldn't accept it and was always looking for him, accosting strangers with searching, distraught eyes and inquiries. Some wanted her put in a home, but Father said she was harmless, just eccentric.

We believed she was a witch.

We brought the weeping Olivia home. Bessie wouldn't let us disturb Mother. She was cross because Jennie was wet all through and she had no sympathy for us.

Father and Aunty May had gone to visit in the next parish and wouldn't be home until late. Olivia continued to weep all that evening and next day. Aunty May got vexed. 'The doll's gone and that's an end of it. We'll buy another when we get home.' But Olivia would not be comforted. Mother heard of it and came to my room where I slept with Olivia. She listened attentively to what we had to tell, sitting on our bed in her flowered silk dressing gown, her dark hair loose and flowing. I thought how very pretty she was.

'I'll be up tomorrow,' she promised, 'and I'll go and see Annie.'

'Oh no, Mammy,' I cried, 'she's a witch.'

'No, she is not,' Mother laughed, 'she's just a lonely old lady. She'll look for the doll if I ask her.'

She went back to bed.

'Oh, she mustn't!' I cried to Olivia. 'See what you've done now. She might never come back. Witches like pretty people. I hate your old doll now.'

I had hitherto been so supportive and sympathetic of Olivia that she was astonished into stopping crying momentarily; then she burst into further tears and wailed, dashing out of my big bed and into her mother's room.

'I want to go home.'

But Aunty May was having a good time – a tennis match had been arranged in Ballycastle and she wasn't going to miss it.

Mother got up the next day, but she was very pale and weak. She sat in the bay window of the drawing-room and looked at the pale blue outline of Rathlin. Father hovered over her and the doctor came again.

I had an idea that frightened me. But I called Olivia.

'We will go, you and I,' I said firmly.

'Where?' she asked.

'To Mad Annie's cottage, of course, and don't tell anyone,' I lowered my voice, 'I don't want Mammy to go. She's not well enough.'

Olivia nodded. 'All right, I'll go with you.'

'Come on then,' I said.

It had been thundering and just as we crept quietly out of the back door of the rectory, clad in our red mackintoshes, sou'westers and Wellington boots, there was a great downpour. We crouched under the meat safe in the yard, shushing one of the dogs who didn't like thunder either. He ran back into the goat's house and glared at us from the hay.

The downpour ceased as suddenly as it had begun. We grabbed hands and ran. Down the rectory fields we raced. Father's tethered goats looked up in surprise, their coats shining as they munched the tall, wet grass, long strands hanging out of their soft, mobile mouths like green beards.

We ran through the stream where we had picnicked and lost the doll, and before our courage could evaporate we continued to run up the side of the next field to a gate. We climbed it and as we dropped over the other side we could see Mad Annie's cottage. We stood still, breathing hard. It was a pretty whitewashed cottage, with a thatched roof, green door and windows, and red and yellow flowers in a window box.

'Doesn't look like a witch's house. Come on.' I edged forward.

We got as far as the white gravel before the cottage and halted. We held hands tight. Olivia kicked the gravel with her toe.

'It's the same as yours,' she whispered.

'So it is,' I looked at the shiny white chippings which sparkled. 'Daddy got ours from White Park Bay.'

We were so absorbed, putting off the moment when

133

we would knock, that we didn't see the door open and a tiny lady come out. When we looked up, there she was smiling at us. She had white hair, a long dark skirt and a red crocheted shawl around her shoulders. She didn't look like a witch at all. I had only seen her in the distance in a long black cloak she wore for outdoors and never got too close because of the stories about her.

She came forward to us. 'Have you come to tea? I hope you have. I love visitors. Come on in.'

She beckoned us to follow her. We hesitated, then gingerly followed her into the cottage. It was as pretty inside as outside. There was a dresser full of cups and saucers, plates and jugs; a high mantelpiece held the same china dogs I had seen in the cottages in the village, a big black clock that ticked loudly and a china bird with very bright colours. There was a real bird in a cage. It was also very bright in colour and it put its head to one side and looked at us, warbling something in a funny high voice.

'That is my friend. He says "Hello" to you. Mr Coots is his name. He's a parrot and that is *his* friend on the mantelpiece.'

I decided there and then that she definitely was not a witch. Witches had crows or ravens for familiars, not friendly parrots.

The little lady was bustling about while she talked, getting a tray and cake tin from the dresser. The kettle was singing as it hung over the peat fire.

'What cups would you like?' the little lady asked, pointing to the dresser. 'You choose. It's nice to have tea out of a cup you like.'

We chose, hesitatingly, with many wondering glances at each other, two pretty cups and saucers covered with roses. Our hostess nodded her approval, her own choice the same.

We sat around a small table sipping our tea and eating fruit cake, silent at first. Then our hostess asked, 'What were you coming to see me about?'

'Olivia lost her doll in the stream. It went under the trees into your field. May we look for it please?'

A strange expression came over her face. 'Lost? Lost? I lost my husband. It's terrible to lose a person you love. Did you love the doll?'

Olivia started to cry.

'Oh, my dear,' cried our hostess, 'I do understand. Of course you may look. I'll come with you. What is the doll's name?'

'Sally,' sobbed Olivia.

'We'll call her name. Come along.'

She pulled the black cape off the back of the door and swept it around her shoulders. Now she looked like a witch, but we knew she wasn't and we weren't frightened of her any more.

We followed her down the field to the stream, much deeper here, shadowed with leaning trees. But there was a broken branch across it and there was Sally, her white baby dress caught in its meshes. We danced with joy and excitement, ready to clamber down the bank into the stream.

'Now, now, keep calm. She will be rescued, never fear,' Miss Annie promised, 'but without another accident. I'll get help. Stay here.'

She went back up the field and through a gate to another cottage. Soon a young man joined her. We recognised Freddie McCann, one of Father's parishioners. He walked straight into the river and pulled Sally to safety. We looked at him with adoration, full of our grateful thanks.

'I'll take them home, Miss Annie,' he said, 'it'll be dark soon.'

We hadn't noticed the light fading.

'Take care of Sally now,' Miss Annie urged; 'don't lose her again.' Her eyes changed. 'I wish I could find my William.'

'Come on now, girls,' Freddie urged, 'we'll go up with Miss Annie and then I'll take you home. Your Mam and Dad'll be worried.'

At the cottage we thanked our new friend for her help and our lovely tea.

'Come again,' she said. 'You are very nice children. I will tell your father.'

There was consternation at home and we were scolded and kissed alternately. 'We didn't want you to go,' I told Mother, 'in case she wouldn't let you home again; that was when I thought she was really a witch,' I ended lamely.

'You were really very brave children,' Mother smiled. She was up and feeling better. We felt better too and glowed with praise. Sally was dried out at the kitchen fire and Bessie made us supper.

'Don't ever do that again,' she admonished. 'You have the heart scalded on me.'

There were tears when Aunty May and Olivia had to go home to Dublin. Mother went in the car with Father this time and took Helen with her. We all stood on the front doorstep in a neat row and had a last photograph taken with Aunty May's Kodak Brownie box camera. The resulting photographs she sent us were a great wonder to us.

It was very dull and quiet at the rectory for a while without them. August ran into September. Then, with preparations for the harvest, a new phase began.

The Threshing

IT WAS A grand treat for me when I was allowed to stay with my friend Cathy who lived about a mile away from the rectory. Even such a little distance away represented an adventure. She was one of a big family who lived on a farm. They were happy-go-lucky and we spent the long end-of-summer days out in the fields, soon now to be gathered and the barns filled for the winter.

We woke up one autumn morning full of anxiety in case the weather had changed. It was only five o'clock when we carefully parted the curtains and eased up the window to lean out. Cathy didn't want us to take her sisters and brothers, younger than she and apt to be a nuisance. Cathy was nine. Her father said that if the dry wind and sun continued they'd gather the big field and begin the threshing today, and we could stay off school to help. All the neighbouring farmers and their labourers would lend a hand, the big hired threshing mill would arrive, and teas at intervals, and lunches, would be delivered to the men all day in the fields, till the harvesting was finished and safe. We'd be running about till the sun went down, as important as everybody else, with nobody to tell us we must go to bed or do our homework. My father was consulted and the teacher would excuse us when we said we were helping with the harvesting. That was how important this day was.

The air was sharp and we knew by the smell of it that

there was going to be another glorious day. The remains of last evening's mist-for-heat was still swelling the shapes of the distant hills and trails of it lingered in the hedges and ditches. Blurred outlines of cows moved and chewed beneath the window. The first birds woke and twittered, gathering answers from far clumps of trees and from the gutter above our heads.

We hadn't long to wait until the household was awake, the smell of bacon coming from the kitchen, the lid of the porridge pots lifting as the already cooked porridge was heaving over the heat. We looked after it, watching the holes appear in the congealed mass, the steam rising from them like the hot springs in New Zealand pictured in my geography book. I pointed them out to Cathy.

'Blurp, glug!' she said delightedly, the wooden spoon ready to stir, making sure it didn't stick and burn. All the family were busy, getting the ordinary everyday tasks out of the way in preparation for the seasonal one, the threshing. After breakfast Cathy's grandmother fed the hens and we helped her, waiting in the run for the birds to come flying through the unbarred entrances for the meal. We loved to tease them, holding the bucket high out of their reach. They'd cluck and fuss around our feet and maybe one or two would fly up to the buckets. Then we'd swing them around and around our heads, sending the birds squawking, and finally throw the golden grain to them in a shower.

We went with the grandmother to collect the eggs, and put them on to boil for the men's lunches. These consisted of fresh soda farls, warm off the griddle, with the butter dripping off them, hard-boiled eggs by the dozen, and tea, boiled in the buttermilk cans and brought to them in the field where they worked. They'd down their forks and throw themselves on the stubble,

sharp though it was, stretch and relax for half an hour, peeling the eggs and filling their mouths with them whole. Then a great bite of hot farl was followed by slurps of tea from the cans. We loved to watch them and could fully sense the extent of the men's need for that food and rest. Because they worked so hard their enjoyment was deeply sensuous, rich and earthy. When they had eaten and drunk they belched loudly, went behind the ricks to relieve themselves, grabbed the older girls and jostled them, or slept briefly in the sun. Then it was back to the gathering again, the rhythm of their movements as they pitched and tossed the sheaves into the thresher mesmerising us as we watched.

There was Willie, the boy from the next farm, aged fifteen, taking his turn up on the thresher, making sure all went in neatly as it came flying off the forks, with a poke here and there before the great jaws clamped down on it. We liked Willie. He was big and strong, but though he looked a man he was still only a boy and shy of the big girls, so at the tea break he'd hoist Cathy on to his shoulders and race around the field with her, leaping the stooks of corn till she squealed with a mixture of delight and fright. Then it would be my turn and he'd never let us fall.

As we sat on a sheaf of corn Cathy's mother threw a tea-cloth over our heads. 'Mind you don't get sunstroke, childer dear.'

Suddenly there was a scream, then another, and another. Men shouted, women came running, covering their faces. The whirring of the thresher was stopped, men climbed on it, the great blades were lifted manually, the men looked down. The silence in the cornfield was different from the silence we had experienced when we had looked out of the bedroom window at five o'clock that morning. Then a man jumped down into the thresher and when he lifted the mangled body another scream pierced the shocked silence and Willie's mother fell to the ground.

We watched the men following the hearse quietly and in orderly twos to the churchyard, and their faces were grave, unlike the faces of the men of the field, and unfamiliar in the dark solemn clothes. The women stood on the doorstep to watch the coffin out of the house and on its last journey, and they wept. The sound of their crying was like a sad song without words. Cathy held her grandmother's hand beneath her black crochet shawl and didn't weep. Since the first screaming that day of the threshing Cathy had neither cried nor spoken. Her brothers and sisters cried noisily with everybody else, except when the horses drawing the hearse came. Then the tears dried on their cheeks while they stared in awe. But Cathy gazed unseeingly at the procession, the black coach with fringed curtains drawn back to reveal the silver-handled coffin and the flowers upon it, the four shining black horses with plumed heads stepping impatiently in the farmyard.

Waiting with the women for the men to come back, Cathy and I helped to set tables, putting out plates of cold meat, cutting up cake. The women stopped weeping and talked, even laughed, and when the men came back they laughed too and cracked jokes and drank and ate, and drank. Now they were more like the men of the field again, with their black ties loosened and their ribald conversation. But Cathy remained silent. Her mother looked at her, concerned.

'She liked Willie but she hasn't shed a tear.'

'She'll be all right when the grieving begins,' said her grandmother.

'But why does she not grieve with us like the other children?'

'Shocked she is, but it is right and natural to grieve. It will come sometime. Let us hope soon.'

But Cathy went about like a little white ghost for a month and only her grandmother was patient.

'Cry, cry, Cathy, for dear sake,' screamed her mother, 'cry for poor Willie.' Cathy only shook her head.

Then one day my mother sent me to keep her company. She was helping to make champ with her grandmother. This was made by simmering chopped scallions in butter and milk and when the boiled potatoes had been put through the masher and were piled high in fine little strings, a hole was made in the middle and the hot mixture poured in. Then it was all beaten together till thick and creamy, dotted again with butter and served alone, needing nothing more to make it a meal for a hungry man. While her grandmother was called away to some other thing Cathy took the big masher down and opened it. Into the sieve she put the freshly boiled potatoes, then grasped the two handles, lowered the hinged mashing plate into the sieve and pressed. Squish! The potatoes were squeezed through the sieve and came out in little white strings ... Cathy hooked one round her finger. It seemed to move and curl, like a worm. She opened the masher and filled it again and pressed the heavy plate down on the potatoes with all her small strength. Out came long wriggling worms. I held one up. 'This is what you're like when you're dead!" I said.

Her grandmother returning heard the screams. The potato masher was on the floor where Cathy had thrown it, open, yawning. Cathy was screaming and pointing at it, tears and potato mixed on her face.

'The thresher ... it's like the thresher ... Oh, poor Willie, poor poor Willie!'

Her grandmother lifted her up.

'She'll be all right now,' she said to the others, gathered at the door. 'The grieving has begun.'

142

The Boat to Rathlin

I WAS DELIGHTED when one day Father had to take a service in the little church of St Thomas on Rathlin Island. The rector of Ballycastle, whose parish included Rathlin, was away on his summer holiday, so Father would fill in for him, and meanwhile a lay preacher would come from Belfast to take Father's normal services for the day. Philippa was sick in bed with a cold, but Father said that I could come with him. I looked happily out of the window at the familiar shape of the island I always referred to as my island.

It was the time of the Lammas Fair in Ballycastle. 'We'll catch the day trippers,' Father said gleefully when he was arranging it.

We set off in the car and I could see a great black cloud rising over Rathlin as we approached Ballycastle harbour. The little town was busy getting ready for the fair. Father knew the stallholder who sold the traditional 'yellow man', a crunchy toffee-like sweet, and dulse, the dried salty seaweed, and he let us buy some even though it was Sunday. Father gave me some and filled his pockets with more for the others when we got back home.

The boat coming from Rathlin seemed to disappear beneath the waves and then bob up again. As it neared the pier I could see several men and a cow on board. I wasn't afraid of cows but this one was behaving wildly, lashing about in the small boat, its eyes enormous with fright. Several men held it with ropes, one tethered to its back legs. The men were shouting and so was the skipper of the boat, which was lurching from side to side, more with the cow's movements than the waves. We stood on the pier waiting to board. I began to feel frightened. Father asked what was the matter that they were bringing a cow to the mainland on a Sunday.

'She's sick,' yelled a man over the noise. 'She has to see the vet, got colic, and she's in calf; don't want to lose her or her calf.'

'Indeed, indeed,' agreed Father going to the steps to offer a hand. 'How'll ye get her up?'

'Just have to pull her up. Mind the child there, yer Reverence, the cow's half crazed with fright and the colic pains.'

Six big men jumped out of the boat while the skipper steadied her against the pier. They began to pull the cow up the slippery steps while more men heaved and pushed from behind.

'Wouldn't you've been better to bring the vet to the cow and her in that state!' exclaimed my father.

'By the time we'd have come for him and he maybe refuse it being a Sunday ... No, we'd no choice. He'll see her all right if we bring her to him. We'll walk her gentle up the road, and Fred here is a mainlander and will keep her in his field till her time is come.'

The exhausted cow finally reached the safety of the quayside and somebody brought her a bucket of water. She drank thirstily and became calmer.

'Daddy, I don't want to go!' I wailed.

'You'll have to. It's too late now,' Father said sternly. 'I have to get to the church for the service. All right, skipper?' he called.

'The boat'd need to be swilled out,' called the skipper. 'It's filthy after that frightened animal.'

'Never mind, it'll have to do, or I'll be late. The people are expecting me. Come on, child.' He was half way down the steps and I had to follow.

The smell in the boat was awful, and as we headed out of the harbour and the first wave heaved, so did my stomach. Further out the waves were enormous. Father sat with me in the stern and held on to me while I threw up all my breakfast and the 'yellow man' over the side. I was sick the whole way across and wondered if I would ever see my mother again. Father made me lie on the hard seat and kept reassuring me that Rathlin was ever getting nearer. I didn't care if I never saw it, and when eventually we reached it and climbed out of the boat in Church Bay I thought it was a most hostile place and vowed to myself that I'd never ever visit it again.

'I'll get her cleaned out for you and the wee lassie, yer Reverence, for coming back,' called the skipper. Mention of the return journey made me feel sick again.

When we reached St Thomas's some of the small congregation came to meet us and Father put me in the charge of a kindly woman.

'Och, the wee white face,' she crooned over me. 'Many's the time that bad sea has nearly had me in its arms for ever. There's no sickness like seasickness. Come on, wee love, lie here.'

She took me into a pew with a padded seat and, taking off my shoes, sat with my feet in her lap, rubbing them gently with warm hands. I was asleep when the service began and heard not one word of it.

When I awoke the sun was shining, and the sand and gravel had taken on a silvery colour. Quite a few visitors had joined us in church: bird watchers and day trippers, weekenders and tourists. I saw that there were two boats bobbing on the waves, waiting for us, but Father and I were invited to lunch near by so we would get a later boat. I looked at the sea and it was still swelling. I couldn't face lunch, but the kindly people coaxed and cajoled.

'The seasickness is never half as bad when you've a lining to the stomach, whereas it will tear at an empty one,' they said, and I had to eat some home-made brown bread and butter and drink a glass of fresh milk. They made a great fuss of me and I stopped looking through the windows to the sea, which had never before been my enemy. Father was cracking jokes with the local people and the Gages, who owned the island. It was the first I learned that the Gages, who lived in Ballycastle, owned the island.

'But I thought God owned it!' I exclaimed indignantly.

'Well,' he laughed, 'He needs folk on earth to administer it, take care of it. The Gages do that very well. There are some in other parts as don't do half as good a job,' he added solemnly.

We were in the boat now and it was clean and the sea was much calmer. On the shore at Ballycastle I looked back at the island, misty blue in the afternoon sunshine.

'Goodbye, Rathlin Island. ... It'll be a long time before I'll visit you again,' I vowed.

Bessie's Wedding

WE COULDN'T BELIEVE it when Bessie said she was leaving us. Mother's health was not good and her departure was a sad blow. But a sect of fundamentalists had come to Dunseverick, and their pastor, an attractive, dynamic young man glowing with the force of his religious fervour, had swept our Bessie off her feet.

Mother said we had to be glad for her. Father glowered. Hitherto the Church of Ireland had been the only church in those parts. The few Presbyterians were big farmers and shopkeepers in and around Bushmills and Ballintoy. Everybody else attended the little stone Church of Ireland church in Lisnagunogue, quietly and unquestioningly. Now the new sect was tearing through the parish like a prairie fire, gathering and scattering all in their stride – 'Mostly gathering,' Father said glumly.

He was aggrieved. He had always brought in a 'hell-fire and brimstone' preacher once a year for a little stimulation. Surely, he thought, that should be enough for, with a few strong reminders from himself in between, his parishioners seemed to wear their hair shirts comfortably enough. Now, however, they were in a ferment of emotional conversion to the new presentation of old truths.

'It'll wear off in time,' he comforted himself; 'it's just the newness.' He thought of several of his parishioners who openly slept in church until he directed his voice straight at them. He'd had to wake Hugh McCann up twice the previous Sunday. No fear of losing him though, he thought, smiling to himself; the loyalty of Hugh McCann and his like was never in question.

But to lose Bessie! It was unthinkable: she was our nurse, our friend. Mother was in bed having another bad day when we were all summoned to her room. On being told that Bessie was leaving to be married the tears of four of us flowed copiously and Jennie joined in even though she didn't know what it was all about. Robert bawled. He'd been Bessie's favourite, if she had a favourite. Mother's tears were quieter.

'Hush, hush,' she comforted, 'we have to be glad for her.'

'There, there,' soothed Bessie, distraught herself.

But it was days, weeks, before the gloom lifted.

Bessie's marriage had other implications. She had become 'saved', and she was intent on saving us. We didn't understand, and I was rebellious.

'I'm baptised. We all are!' I protested.

Bessie told us tales of hell-fire, provoking visions of the Devil stoking them.

'Where does the Devil get the turf?' Philly asked, and Father told his colleagues, other clergy with similar poaching problems. The joke of it lifted their spirits. Nevertheless, he began to be worried at Bessie's efforts to frighten us into being saved.

'I'm an inheritor of the Kingdom of Heaven!' I yelled in an argument with Bessie, whom I now began to see through less-than-rose-tinted spectacles. She told me that everybody who wasn't saved went to hell and there was no second chance. I was frightened and told her it was most unfair. Father had a word with her and there was an end to the lurid descriptions of the torture of the damned. For my part I sang 'Jesus Loves

Me' in defiant tones whenever she was within hearing distance.

All the same, I was thrilled when Bessie asked me to be her bridesmaid. Her young man had wanted to take her away up to Belfast to get married, but she wanted my father to marry her. She had no relations except an old grandmother who couldn't travel. We were the nearest thing to being her relations. So she insisted and won the day.

Mother set about making a dress for her, and they both went into Coleraine, taking me with them, to buy the material. Father drove us and then left us to look around the shops while he went to have lunch with the rector of Coleraine. We were excited and happy on our own around the shops. We chose pale blue silky material for Bessie's dress and little pink and lilac flowers for mine. Bessie also had to have a hat and favoured wheat-coloured straw. Mother said she'd trim it with the material of her dress. White shoes and gloves were added and Bessie's eyes shone.

I hated hats but Mother said I'd have to wear one. There wasn't much money left out of what Father had given us and we wanted to treat ourselves to lunch in a restaurant.

'There are flowers to be got,' Mother said doubtfully, counting the money in her purse.

'I want a bunch of sweet pea out of the rectory garden,' Bessie announced.

Mother's eyes lit up. 'Oh, won't that be lovely: there are such a lot and the colours are glorious. And Vivien can wear her white panama hat with some of them to dress it up.'

She was so pleased that I had to be too. And now there would be enough money for lunch.

'After all, Daddy is getting his free,' she giggled girlishly, as we settled around a table in a smart restaurant. It was wonderful to see her feeling and looking so much better than she had been for months. It must, I concluded, be the excitement of the wedding. Bessie smiled happily at her.

The wedding day morning dawned fine and bright. Bessie had a bath and washed her hair and I brushed it for her until it shone. It was brown and luxuriant and she had trouble making her hat stay on, but Mother found a hat-pin and there was no breeze to blow it off. She looked lovely, her eyes bluer in the reflection of the dress. It was beautifully made and fitted by Mother. I rammed my panama hat on resentfully but had to admit that when Mother added the sweet pea trimming it improved both the hat and me.

In the quiet little church Mother played the Bridal March, even though Bessie didn't want to walk up the aisle as she had no male relation to give her away. Her feeble old grandmother was sitting in a back seat just inside the door, glad that she could walk that far. So Bessie and I followed Father slowly out of the vestry to where the groom was standing at the chancel steps. I looked at the best man: I knew I'd have to walk out down the aisle with him. He was small and had curly red hair and he turned and winked at me. It was so mischievous a wink that I shook with barely controlled giggles until well into the ceremony.

Suddenly Father asked, 'Who giveth this woman to this man?'

There was silence. No answer came. I saw Mother shaking her head at Father but he wasn't looking. He asked again, 'Who giveth this woman to this man?' in just the same stern voice he asked Bible questions in Sunday school.

I couldn't stand the tension. There must be some answer.

'God!' I blurted out.

Father seemed suddenly to be in a fluster; his shoulders under the full white surplice shook and his prayer book fell to the chancel steps. As he bent to retrieve it the young pastor smiled and nodded approvingly at me and the best man winked elaborately and solemnly again. Mother had disappeared behind the organ, and Father had an unusually red face and watery eyes as he continued with the service.

There was a little reception in the school hall, put on for Bessie by all the people in the parish who knew her and loved her as much as we did. There were flowers and little tables covered with hand-embroidered table-cloths, and borrowed best tea-sets. A wedding cake stood on the big table where we, the bridal party, sat. Father sat with us as he had to make a speech, and Mother shared a little table with Philippa, Helen and Robert. Jennie sat on Mother's knee, and kept pointing at me and screeching, 'Fifee! Fifee!' for she was too small to be able to pronounce my name. But nobody minded.

I had the best man beside me and when he rose to make his speech he said I was the nicest bridesmaid whose health he ever had the honour to propose, 'and the cleverest,' he added, 'to come up with such an answer at a moment's notice,' and everybody roared laughing. But a little lingering doubt entered my mind, a little uneasy feeling, and later I asked Father.

'Daddy, was that the right answer?'

'Not quite, daughter dear, but a very good one nevertheless. It was my fault anyway. I forgot to leave that bit out, for Bessie's sake.'

'It wasn't a *faux pas*, Daddy, was it?'

We'd been learning French in school and I knew that a *faux pas* was unpardonable.

'Oh no, sweetheart, there's never a *faux pas* committed in church. God wouldn't be bothered with such nonsense.'

I was comforted.

To replace Bessie, which Mother said despondently could never be done, a succession of maids came. One stayed a month and was promising, learning avidly from Mother how to lay a table and wait on it, and then went off to Portrush where she wanted to be a waitress in a big hotel. A sweet little lame girl called Linda came and we were beginning to love her when Father learned that she had TB of the knee. She was dismissed with more tears. Mother became more and more tired and was more frequently confined to bed. Katie came puffing up from the village regularly. She was an enormous woman, clad in a voluminous black skirt with a red flannel one underneath, a huge white apron on top and a black knitted shawl. She wore black woollen stockings held up around her knees with elastic bands, and no knickers.

'Unhealthy,' she avowed when I protested, shocked, after seeing her squat in the henhouse, caught short while gathering the eggs.

Katie was good to us in her way, always washing and ironing what she called our 'simmets and drawers', little bodices all tapes and buttons for holding up our stockings, and knickers with elastic or cuffs around the legs. Father's surplices frightened her, and she put us all out of the kitchen while she spread the voluminous white vestment over the deal table which was covered with a blanket and then a spotless white sheet. The flat irons heating on the range had to be spotless too, spat on and rubbed for heat and cleanliness before use. Nothing must spoil this holy garment.

When Mother had to go to a nursing home in Belfast it became an ordeal for us all. Father was having financial worries and was cross. Mother and Father had not been sleeping in the same bed for some time now, not even in the same room. I asked Katie about this. She looked at me curiously as if to say my tongue was too long again, then answered kindly enough.

'Your Mam is not to have any more babies, doctor's orders.'

I had to be satisfied with that. Togetherness, it seemed, meant babies.

We started to go to school in Coleraine, though Mother tried to persuade Father that the Bushmills school was good enough and would shorten the journey for him. He wouldn't hear of it. The Coleraine school was the best, and to it we travelled daily, even though Robert was the only boy in the kindergarten. We often arrived late, later than ever now with Mother in hospital in Belfast. Katie came very early, red-faced with exhaustion from the walk from the village, to make our breakfasts and put up school lunches. The thick white slices of loaf bread were slabbed together with jam and cut into four. She wrapped them up in any available paper, often wallpaper, for paper was scarce.

Mother came home inside a month. She had been supposed to stay longer but she was homesick, missing us all too much. She couldn't walk very well and she sat in a chair by her bed a great deal, but she smiled again as she looked through the windows at Rathlin and the tumbling clouds. The seagulls and guillemots wheeled and whirled over the house and out to sea. She was home.

Then one winter's day she and I were together in her

big bed. We were both sick, she with rheumatic fever again and me with a kidney complaint. I wasn't allowed any food, only drinks of the water off boiled barley, which was horrible and slimy. I was starving and miserable, but there was no use complaining to Father who was cross again. He had to go away for a weekend and ordered both of us not to move out of our room until he came back. Mother looked at him pleadingly and he looked sternly back at her.

'It's for the good of your health, Connie,' was all he said. I was puzzled, but Mother turned away and shut her eyes when he was gone.

When he came back he was in high spirits. We were off for the school holidays at Christmas, and the others were all playing in the dining-room where a little shelved pantry off it afforded our fertile imaginations a great shop. It was full of Mother's best china and we were allowed to play with the delft on the lower shelves and solemnly promised not to touch any other. I was still in bed wailing with hunger and longing to be playing shop with the others. Father bounded upstairs and kissed Mother and me.

'We are moving to Ardglass in County Down in the spring,' he said.

Mother tried not to let him see the tears, so ready to fall.

'That'll give you two time to get well, and the weather in County Down is much milder than up here. It'll be better for you. Wait until you see how much better you'll feel.'

Mother couldn't smile and he chided her.

'I'll be a rector, no longer just a curate-in-charge. It means more money, schools for the children. There's an excellent co-ed in Downpatrick. They need to meet more children of their own age. They can go on the train every day. Then the primary school is next door to the rectory for Robert and Jennie. And the rectory is beautiful – an old, long, low plantation house. You'll love it.'

'Will there be Catholics in Ardglass?' I asked, always curious.

'It's mostly Catholic,' Father answered. 'We'll be the minority, but everybody gets on fine and the local priest is from my place, Dalkey. We'll be friends. The industry is fishing; there's a great smell of herrings.'

It was Mother's weakness that made her weep. 'I'm glad for you, Bertie, you know I am. It will be all right, right for us all. I just wish I was well.'

'You will be, you will be,' he held her in his arms, then looked at me as I cried into my pillow.

'May God give me patience!' he exclaimed. 'There's nothing but snivelling in this house. Come on, big girl, dry your eyes, childhood is over,' and he went downstairs to tell the others.

Philly was so astonished that she dropped a soup tureen with a crash. It was one of the delft ones out of our 'shop'. Father roared at her and she raced upstairs to join the rest of us in Mother's bedroom.

Soon we began to sense an adventure in store. Robert was only worried about bringing his livestock with him. He had a mouldy rabbit and a hedgehog that lived in a nest under a hedge, as well as a host of creepy-crawly things that lived in matchboxes. Mother reassured him. Philippa and Helen thought it would be fun to go to school on a train, and although I felt very sick I thought that meeting some boys other than my brother might be interesting.

By this time we had found a new live-in maid we all liked, from Dervock out in the country towards Ballycastle. She was as fond of Mother as Bessie had been. When she heard the news she comforted us and

Mother by promising to come to Ardglass with us, 'for a month or two until you get someone else and are settled in'. Mother began to cheer up.

That winter was a bad one, with mists so thick that Rathlin was blotted out and the surrounding hillsides lost to view and we felt as though we were on an island ourselves. Only Rathlin's two red eyes and lonely fog horn's moan reminded us of its presence. Few boats ventured out, and fish was scarce. Even huge log fires in the rectory and one in Mother's bedroom did little to dispel the damp and cold. The pump in the yard froze and we had no water. Father borrowed a blowlamp and unfroze enough of it to get a small bucket of drinking water, but the toilet wasn't functioning and the clothes could not be washed. The village houses had dry outside toilets and our dear friend Jane invited us to her house for the daily routine. I thought I'd die of the cold sitting in her little wooden shed on a hole in a board over an even bigger hole in the ground, with the wind whistling up and freezing my bottom. Mother was afraid I'd get another chill on my kidneys so I had to use the chamber pot, which was emptied into a bucket and carried to the cesspit where all the stinging nettles grew at the bottom of one of the rectory fields. I felt that horrible place was full of bad goblins and maybe even the Devil himself lived there.

So when the spring came and we began to get ready for the move, we were glad that such winters were behind us. Mother agreed that she couldn't stand another. The parishioners were disappointed and sad. They understood the weather: it comes and it goes, they'd say with resignation.

One spring day I went with Father to the slough, as it was known, a deep pool in the rocks at Dunseverick village, and here he swam while I clambered over the rocks and sand. It was too cold for me to go into the water but Father was a powerful swimmer and swam in all weathers. I found a stick, long and pointed, and while I waited for Father to dress I doodled on the sand. Away in the distance I could see the house amidst green fields and brown freshly ploughed ones, the avenue of trees etched against the sky. A boat was bobbing on the waves. I drew the house and the boat on the sand, then added a bird flying over. I could hear birds calling, swooping after fish and then soaring high into the blue, cloud-filled sky. I was leaving it all. My eyes were full of tears as I saw Father coming. He bent over, his hands on his knees, and looked into my woe-begone face. I continued to hang my head, watching through the blur of tears the frilled lace edge of the waves beginning to wipe out the picture I had drawn.

Then Father said, 'Put all these memories of your young life here in a little box in the back of your head. Some day you can take them out and they will give you pleasure. Come on now, no looking back. You don't want to be turned into a pillar of salt like Lot's wife!'

I didn't indeed. I turned to him, sniffing, without a handkerchief.

'That's it girl: on, on, to "fresh fields and pastures new".'

Suddenly he did a little jig on the sand and broke into the words of 'Phil the Fluter's Ball'.

'Oh, hadn't we the gaiety
at Phil the Fluter's ball!'

I knew he was trying to make me laugh and I resisted as long as I could, but he looked so funny capering there, his trousers gathered up around his ankles with bicycle clips, his boots kicking up the sand, that I gave in, threw away my stick, burst into laughter and followed him.

Epilogue

PHILIPPA AND I went to Dunseverick once more when she came again to Ireland. We had heard a rumour that someone had rented the rectory from the church, after it had lain idle, the young newspaper men long gone, and it was in need of repair. Indeed, as a family we had thought of renting it between us for holidays, but we couldn't have afforded to carry out all the repairs it needed, nor could the church.

We were unprepared for what we saw.

'It's all poshed up!' I exclaimed. It had turned into a mansion.

Everything was shining new: even the coachhouse had been renovated, a new garage had been built, and there was a sun porch; the avenue had gone, replaced by a wide tar macadamed approach. No trees.

'No tree house,' Philippa remarked.

We read a shiny new plaque on the cream-washed wall beside the gate. 'The Old Rectory', it said. There were cream walls where hedges had been, the ground had been terraced. No daisy field.

Oddly, Mother's ornamental pedestals were still there, beside the front door. Antiques now, I supposed.

The new people came to the windows and looked at us.

'We'd better go,' Philippa tugged at my arm.

'They're all gone,' I sighed.

'Who?'

159

'The ghosts. Mother, Father, Bessie ...' I gazed around me with a strange emptiness. 'I won't come again.'

'Well come on now,' Philippa was impatient, 'you're making me feel creepy. Gee, it's some improvement, better than letting it go into disrepair. I bet the new people enjoy that view.'

It was indeed glorious, a day of blue distances, sunshine sparkling on the water, Rathlin still lying like a basking shark.

'Have you written it all down yet?' Philippa asked as we drove away. 'You've got grandchildren. Tell them.'